Jack

The Christmas Collie

Kevin L. Brett
Stafford, Virginia

This book is a work of fiction, based on a real Collie, Captain Jack.

Publisher's Cataloging-In-Publication Data
(Prepared by The Donohue Group, Inc.)

Brett, Kevin L.
  Jack : The Christmas Collie / Kevin L. Brett.

   p. : ill. ; cm.

   ISBN-13: 9780981935010
   ISBN-10: 098193501X

1. Fiction-Animal stories. 2. Dogs. 3. Children's books.
 I. Title.

PCIP Pending
NNN.N   2009909902

ATTN: Quantity discounts are available to your company educational institution, government agency or organization.

For more information, please contact the author at Kevin Brett Studios, Inc.
19 Live Oak Lane, Stafford, Virginia 22554 540-845-4755
sales@KevinBrettStudios.com

Kevin Brett
STUDIOS

Education | Entertainment | Family

www.KevinBrettStudios.com

Dedication

To my children William, Alexandra and Samantha. Always remember that when we give, we also receive, and the gifts that we give can be life changing.

Kevin L. Brett

JACK'S STORY

Kevin L. Brett

Author's Foreword

Christmas Eve, 2008
Stafford, Virginia

On a cold winter's night two thousand years ago, the course of humanity changed forever. The world received a precious child. That night, he was spared the terrible fate suffered by the other sons of Bethlehem at the hand of Herod's soldiers. Through the gift of this child, the world has learned the true meaning of giving and sacrifice.

Two Christmases ago, a certain Collie entered our family. That Collie's life was spared a terrible fate by a choice that we made. We changed the course of his life and he has changed ours. Through him, we have had the opportunity to practice the lesson of that first Christmas.

We always have choices; some easy; some involving sacrifice. Sacrifice can be enlightening and life changing. While it may seem unappealing at first, in the end, it is a blessing when you make that sacrifice and give of yourself. Each of us carries this gift inside. The choice to use it is ours.

Merry Christmas!

Kevin Brett

Kevin L. Brett

Prologue: An Ancient Breed

Jack's is an ancient story that you could say actually begins eons ago in the fascinating and mysterious land of Scotland. The Scottish Highlands are a harsh, yet beautiful landscape that was formed nearly three billion years ago. In an ancient and distant era, Scotland had been attached to its mother continent; what is now North America. The Scottish land mass had broken free and during the ensuing eons, began a slow, but certain, collision course with another land mass that had also separated from its mother continent. That other land mass was the current isle of Great Britain. The British isle had been adjoined to the European mainland, but due to geologic forces, and through the medium of time, it too had broken off from its parent and gradually headed west, away from the mainland. These two gigantic ocean-going vessels finally met in violent confrontation 350 million years before the present day. The Scottish isle crashed into the British isle, smashing, unyieldingly, against its northern coast and wrinkling the landscape to create the rugged mountains and harsh terrain that is now the beautiful and mystical Scottish Highlands. Only a similarly endowed breed of dog such as the Collie could be born of such environs.

After the end of the last ice age, about twelve thousand years ago, immense glaciers left deep scars on the land. These depressions filled with frigid, melting glacier water, forming lochs or lakes. Around 7000 B.C., man first ventured from Europe to Britain and north into Scotland. These intrepid souls were nomads; hunter-gatherers. They survived on animals they caught, wild berries, grains, roots, fruits and shellfish.

As Scotland became more heavily forested over the centuries, the large game animals such as bison and wildebeest could not survive without open land to roam and graze. They began to die out, and a large food source for these Mesolithic hunters began to disappear. As the Neolithic age began, around 4000 B.C., the hunters started to supplement their diet with food that they had grown. They were learning farming, and they began to establish permanent settlements. In the following centuries, farmers and herders brought both seed and livestock from the European mainland. Along with this livestock came a variety of dogs with varying herding abilities. During the following ages, this land would be settled by Celts, invaded by Vikings and conquered by Romans; each bringing their own contributions, and each leaving a permanent mark on Scotland and its history.

Hunters began to interact with wolves, which began to follow them. Eventually, these wolves became somewhat domesticated, in that they stayed near the hunters and even helped in the hunt, sensing that somewhere in the contract was a clause that entitled them to a portion of the spoils.

The dogs of these new immigrating or invading peoples occasionally bred with some of the more docile of these "friendly" wolves, and new more domesticated dogs or wolves emerged. While wolves are hunters and pack animals, the dogs had been bred to be herders for the cattle and other livestock. These new dogs exhibited the intense loyalty of a wolf to his pack, the keen senses and hunting instincts of the wolf, along with the protective nature of dogs watching over their herds.

A Celtic term emerged for these hard-working, tough dogs – colley: meaning useful. It also referred to both their black color and the black-faced sheep known as colleys or Collies that these dogs herded so successfully. These dogs were black and white and rather small, generally 25-45 pounds, and were later bred with Irish setters to increase their size and to give them straighter legs. They were crossed with the Gordon Setter to increase the tan color so they could be differentiated at a distance from their sheep. They were also bred with the Borzoi to increase the size of the head and their intelligence. Shepherds believed that the runts of the litter were more intelligent – having to learn how to survive and prosper amidst their larger siblings. They would breed the runts to increase the intelligence of these dogs.

Collies were used to herd and guard their sheep, cattle, goats and pigs. As the wool industry flourished in England and Scotland, breeding valuable Collie sheep dogs was critical to the success of this industry. Shepherds needed a dog that was powerful and rugged and could run 20-40 miles in a day, herding sheep over long distances. These Collies had to be intelligent and able to think on their own, as they often would work the flocks of sheep a long ways away from any assistance shepherds might be able to offer. A Collie had to be able to round up stray sheep, return them to the flock, keep watch for predators, such as their wolf ancestors, and move the sheep down the mountain or across pastures, to new grazing lands, or to market, with only minimal contact with their shepherds.

These dogs developed in different regions of England and Scotland began to take on the names of their regions, yielding such breeds as Northern Sheepdogs, Highland Collies, Welsh Sheepdogs, Shetland Sheepdogs, Scotch Collies and others.

These working dogs suddenly were thrust into canine celebritydom in the late 1800s, when Queen Victoria took a fancy to them. She was known actually to keep a group of Collies at her summer palace at Scotland's Balmoral Castle. Everyone in England began to gravitate rapidly toward this new royally sanctioned breed. In 1860 a Collie was exhibited in the Birmingham Dog Show in the class "Scotch Sheep Dogs". Old Cockie placed second out of fourteen. Most show Collies trace their pedigree back to Old Cockie, or his grandson Charlemagne who was a sable and white Collie.

In 1879, the first English Collie was imported to the United States, and breeders began developing the breed to a slightly larger size with more refined features and temperament. Between 1900 and 1930, the Collie continued to grow in popularity through the books of Albert Peyson Terhune and his stories of his Sunnybank Collies of New Jersey. In 1938, Eric Knight wrote a short story about Lassie for the Saturday Evening Post, and in 1940, he released the book, *Lassie Come Home*, which was followed by the movie of the same title in 1943. The 1943 hit was followed by six sequels and a television series that ran from 1954 through 1971. This series was followed still by several more feature films.

Kevin L. Brett

Beginnings: 7000 BC

She paced nervously near the edge of the forest, keeping behind a low bush to conceal her position. Her exquisite sense of smell tuned in to the aroma of meat cooking over an open fire. The fire added a natural condiment of smoky flavor and scent to this winter meal in the making. The small family of primitive Mesolithic hunters gathered in their simple hut fashioned of wood framing and covered in red deer and bison hide. They slowly turned the large hunks of bison meat over a spit.

This band of primitives were among the first to make their way across retreating glaciers that connected what is now Great Britain and Scotland to the main continent of Europe. They had followed migrating bison, red deer, bears and giant elk. Tonight these hunters were busily contented, knowing that their meal for this frigid winter evening would soon be ready. The gray wolf did not share the hunter's enthusiasm.

She and her mate had recently left their pack to strike out on their own. With food supplies scarce for the winter, the male had separated from the female nearly a week ago in an attempt to find prey to bring back to his mate. Some ill fate must have befallen him since their separation. She, being left to fend entirely for herself, had not had any success finding even the smallest prey to sustain her. She was becoming weak, and it was difficult to stay warm. She could feel the numbing cold beginning to penetrate her thick fur. Her body was simply not producing enough heat due to the lack of food that normally would keep her warm in such circumstances. In another month, it would be mating season, and they would have been starting a litter of Scottish Highland gray wolves, but tonight her only thoughts were on the hunger pangs that she felt deep inside, as she stalked beneath the twinkling stars of the cold, cloudless, winter night sky.

The wolf was almost delirious with hunger, as she paced now closer, just beyond the visual protection of the brush that she had only a moment ago hidden behind. Her submissive and trusting nature allowed her to take a chance that the hunters would be too busy to notice if she inched closer to catch a better sample of the scent that drifted through this frigid night air. Her hunting instincts told her that maybe; just maybe, there might be some remnants of the hunter's bounty lying around the periphery of the camp. Surely, the hunters were too caught up in reveling over their victory. After all, taking down a bison is no small feat, and these highland hunters knew they would be going to sleep with full bellies tonight, so they had no immediate worries or cares.

The campsite flickered from the glow of the campfire emanating from within, as the gray female canis lupus inched slightly closer to the primitive encampment. She focused on the spit of turning meat that she could now see through a small opening in one of the larger huts. Her gaze was transfixed on the meat glowing above the embers and the lapping flames of the hunter's fire. She was weary from the cold and her gnawing hunger. She sensed no real threat from these humans, especially since they were new to the area, and she had not previously had any experience that would lead her to believe they represented any type of threat.

She lay down on a patch of bare earth encircled by a small, crescent shaped mound. The mound served to block some of the occasional biting wind while still affording her a view of the food. Why she lay there, now within plain sight of the main hut and a mere few yards from its entrance, she did not know. It almost did not matter. She could at least smell the food. As she drifted out of consciousness, it seemed to become eerily quiet. Were the hunters finally settling down for the evening so that she might begin to search for a few possible scraps, or was she fading slowly into unconsciousness from a combination of exhaustion, brought on by the intense cold and lingering hunger?   Her thoughts were blurred. Her senses were dulled, and then after some unknown moments or seconds, her next sensation was the feel of a gentle caress.

Far back in her memory, she recalled a vague sensation that she must have felt as a wolf cub, nestling near her mother and siblings, having her coat cleaned by the gentle caress of her mother's tongue. Her lapping caress continued for a few more strokes, before her senses were heightened by this gentle stimulation, and she momentarily returned back to what seemed like a more conscious state. It was not her mother; not her wolf mother. It was one of those humans; a female, she sensed. A creature with sensitivities not that dissimilar from her own, was knelt down gently caressing her head and her coat. She felt no threat. Her already opened eyes dull with weariness, focused a bit more clearly in the darkness, and for a fleeting moment, void of fear, the two creatures exchanged a gaze.

The human pushed a bone, ripe with juicy meat, toward the wolf's mouth. The wolf sniffed it, focused her senses on it, and slowly and gently, with her waning strength, chewed and savored the meat. She was so singularly focused on the seemingly magical appearance of this gift that any sense of threat or need for flight had left her. For that brief moment, she ate while the human sat motionless, holding the bone by its end and affording the wolf easy access to the ample meat that surrounded it.

Something was happening. The shared gaze and the trusting sense of this female wolf were amplified by her weariness, combined with the offering from this human. The wolf's intense loyalty to its pack seemed almost transmuted across the biological barrier of species to this other female. Some indescribable bond was being forged, which neither creature understood, but which made both acutely aware of this moment of mutual trust. This wolf was supplicating its security and its trust upon this other female. The human gently let the bone down on the ground in front of the wolf as she continued to eat calmly. The human slowly stood up and backed away. The wolf paused and simply gazed in silent appreciation and acceptance of this "friend", before continuing to strip the bone clean.

The wolf and her offspring frequented the camp boundaries and continued to have occasional chance encounters with, not only the females, but also other members of this human group. With time, a trusting bond developed. Later generations of this wolf's offspring experienced similar encounters, and in fact, looked upon these humans, not as prey or threats, but as neighbors in this otherwise harsh community. These wolves followed, as the nomads moved in search of game. The wolves were present as these humans began to establish permanent settlements.

Today there are no wolves in Scotland. They have been hunted to extinction. Most historians agree with the account that the last wolf in Scotland was killed by a hunter named MacQueen, in 1743, near the Findhorn River, in the territory of the tribal clan Mackintosh.

There is a current movement to reintroduce wolves to Scotland to help cull the immense red deer population, which numbers in the hundreds of thousands. These deer cause damage to crops, forests and neighboring animal habitats. Without the presence of wolves to keep their numbers in check, the deer will continue to wreak significant environmental and economic stress. The Collie, however, has prospered and is still used for its original purposes and continues to carry the characteristics inherited from its wolf ancestors.

Chapter 1
Dogs Just Help Kids Grow Up Right

The Barnes children were in the family room watching the most recent Lassie movie for the umpteenth time. There was a pivotal scene where a family on a road trip encountered a stray Collie at a roadside dinner. The son and daughter in the movie pleaded with the parents to let them adopt the dog and take the beautiful sable and white Collie with them to their new home in the country. "Please Dad," implored the daughter, "We need a dog. Besides, dogs just help kids grow up right."

It didn't take many re-enactments of that scene in the Barnes home, before Keith and Linda realized that it was time. They needed a dog too. Why? Well because, like the movie said, dogs just help kids grow up right.

"You know the kids are at a perfect age now," said Keith, as he and Linda settled into bed that evening after watching the Lassie movie.

"But what type of dog are we going to get?" queried Linda. "You know I'm not crazy about a lot of shedding, and Collies shed," she continued.

"They don't shed all the time, and besides, I'll help groom him and teach the kids that they have to help groom him as well," defended Keith.

Keith and Linda were both in their early forties and had three very energetic children, Sandra, four, Allie, six and Wesley, nine. Linda and Keith were both very committed and involved in shaping and growing their children. They lived in a pleasant neighborhood in North Stafford, nestled in a forested region of the county marked by a series of small valleys and ridges. They had lived there since the neighborhood was built and had seen many families come and go. So, after eleven years in the same house, Keith and Linda felt like they were winning the marathon of home ownership, relative to many of the other families on their street.

Keith was a leader for Wes's Boy Scout Troop, and Linda was a leader for the girl's Girl Scout Troop. Linda was a substitute teacher at Winding Creek Elementary, which both girls attended, and Keith was an IT professional for a large defense contractor. Keith and Linda also spent considerable time taxiing their three children to various other activities such as soccer, football, gymnastics and church events. In many ways, they were a typical suburban family.

Sandra was a cutie, with long, silky, rich brown hair that flowed all the way down her back. Her brown locks outlined her adorably freckled, creamy white face. Allie, who was barely an inch taller than her baby sister, had bright blond hair with fair complexion and pretty, green eyes. Wesley, was tall and thin like his father. Wes had an engaging smile and straight, but somewhat wispy, dark brown hair and bright eyes that readily revealed his inquisitive and passionate nature. They were all bright, caring and sweet kids who would thoroughly enjoy and love their new pet. The Barnes children had wanted a dog, cat, or something, for a couple of years, but Linda wanted to make sure that the girls were old enough.

"Sandra is old enough now. It's not like she's a baby any more, and Allie and Wes need a dog. We don't want Wes getting any older than he is now, or he'll miss out on the whole growing up with a dog experience if we wait until he's twelve or fourteen. We have to get one while they're still young," retorted Keith emphatically.

"I know. You're right," conceded Linda. "I just couldn't see getting a dog earlier when the girls were two or three. That would have just been too much of a handful to have two little girls still in diapers and trying to manage with a new puppy. It would be hard to handle that much while you're gone at work during the day. You know I'll be the one who has to take care of him."

Kids have a funny way of instantly becoming responsible, grown-up and mature when they think they stand a good chance of getting what they want. They talk about how they will take care of any new pet that the parents should agree to welcome into their home, and then suddenly, when it's time to clean the droppings, feed the pet or take it for a walk, a magical thing happens; they go back to being kids - instantly. They have no interest in tending to the mundane daily chores that come with owning and raising a pet. Somehow, magically, all those promises, made in a moment of weakness, were as if they had never even been uttered. Of course, Keith and Linda possessed ample amounts of parental clairvoyance, and through these magical powers, knew that was how the scene would play out in the Barnes home.

So, it was settled, but what type of dog would it be? Cats were out. Both Keith and Linda preferred the companionship and loyalty of dogs, versus the independent nature of cats.

"I've always loved Golden Retrievers," suggested Linda. "I'm not too crazy about really small dogs. They make me think of some type of rodent. Ya have to be able to hug 'em," she said.

"So we want a larger dog," Keith declared. Both were thinking of some type of larger breed with which they and the kids could wrestle and play.

"Also, it would be good to have a guard dog to protect the family," said Linda.

Keith had grown up with a beautiful and humongous, rusty red Collie named after the famous Macintosh apple; not the computer, the fruit. Keith had also grown up watching the Lassie movies. Like the rest of the world, he fell in love with the brave, loyal and highly intelligent dog. Having one in his family at age five, he still remembered the magnificent Collie and the thick lion-like coat of fur. Later, in his teen years, Keith's family had a sable and white Collie – Piney Branch Lindsay Lad. Piney Branch referred to the breeder, and Lindsay Lad was the obligatory Scottish name. It is almost mandatory, or at least should be, for any Collie owner who knows anything about this wonderful breed to endow them with a Scottish name.

It was settled. It would be a Collie. Keith let Linda discuss other possible types of dogs to make her feel part of the process of deciding which type to choose. He was flexible on almost anything, but when it came to dogs; hands down, he loved Collies, and he was long overdue for another.

Carol had to quit her teaching job because she had a rare medical condition which caused tremors and seizures, and the frequency of them was increasing. The doctors had actually said that the seizures could be controlled by drinking fresh goat milk on a regular basis. Apparently, it contained a particular type of protein, which, for some unknown reason, prevented the seizures. Of course, fresh goat milk is not something that can be routinely purchased at your neighborhood grocer, unless you live in some place like the highlands of Scotland, and you have a heard of goats, protected, of course, by several Collies.

Moving to Scotland wasn't an option, but buying a small farm in central Virginia was. Carol and her husband, who was also a teacher, purchased a thirty-acre farm called Sunrise Acres. The farm had a quaint farmhouse in the middle of the property. It came with six healthy horses, a good number of chickens, a well-used pickup truck and goats.

After moving to Sunrise Acres, it wasn't long before Carol and her husband Mark discovered one of the slightly less appealing facets of farm ownership; snakes. In this part of Virginia, there were frequent visits by poisonous Copperhead snakes. Carol had read that certain types of dogs were particularly skilled at fending off snakes and protecting livestock and their owners. In fact, that certain type of dog was the Collie. Collies, by their protective nature, watch out for their flock or their pack, be it their human family, chickens, or whatever.

Carol and Mark had been referred through some new friends to Michael Billingston a retired Collie breeder. They had met a friendly local couple while on a weekly trip to the local general store in the nearby town of Johnson's Corner. The couple introduced Carol and Mark to Mr. Billingston. He offered to give them some tips about controlling their snake problem. Michael had spent thirty years breeding and developing Collies for the dog show circuit. He knew the noble breed well and knew that, for centuries, the Collie had been versatile and easily trainable.

One Saturday afternoon, Carol decided to call Michael.

"Hello, Mr. Billingston?"

"Yes," he answered.

"Hi. This is Carol Walker. We met at the general store."

"Oh. Yes. How are you?"

"Very well, thanks. I thought I would call and see if, possibly, you had any Collies for sale. My husband Mark and I decided that we'd like to take you up on your

25

advice to buy some Collies for the farm to help out with the snake problem," she continued.

"Great. Well, if you have some time tomorrow afternoon, why don't you come by my farm and see what we have?"

"That would be perfect. We'll see you then."

The next day, Carol and Mark met with Michael. He recommended that it might be wise to have two male Collies, so the grounds of Sunrise Acres would be well protected. Carol and Mark agreed, but there was a catch. Carol had spotted a particularly striking tri-color Collie. She was mesmerized by the little ball of fur and couldn't take her eyes off of it. Michael had selected two outstanding male puppies, who in just a few months, would become very good protectors of the property at Sunrise Acres, but Carol was also in love with the tri-color named Penny; a girl. Penny's coat was jet black and glistened in the sunlight, while her snow-white ruff glowed as it reflected the intensity of the sun. The sable coloring in the face, fore and rear paws added a splash of richness to Penny's color palette, creating a stunning effect.

Tri-color Collies are identical in marking to the more familiar sable and white of Lassie fame, but where the sable and white has the tan or sable colors covering most of their body, the tri-color has black in place of the sable. The tri-color's face has small tan patches above the eyes like a mask and a mostly tan and white muzzle, white chest and white ruff around the neck, white paws and a tail of black with a white tip. The tri-color is a black and white version of Lassie, with sable accents much like the original Colleys.

One of the males was Bully, a noble-looking blue merle. The blue merle, by contrast, is predominately several rich shades of grey, and the remainder, such as the chest, paws and ruff, is white; all three, Collies through and through and all three variations equally stunning and magnificent to behold.

"I have to have Penny," said Carol. "She's beautiful! You can take Bully and Lance as the main defenders against snakes, but Penny will be my girl," she finished.

So Sunrise Acres now had a trio of Collie pups who were about to take charge and run the farm. Little did Carol and Mark know how much the three Collies would transform the landscape and the population of Sunrise Acres.

Several months passed, and the three Collies found their stride. Penny, Bully and Lance owned Sunrise Acres, but they did everything possible to make Carol and Mark feel at home. When it comes to herding dogs such as the Collie, humans do not own them. The dogs own the humans; they are the dog's flock at times and their pack at other times. This seemingly schizophrenic behavior stems from the mixture of wolf pack pride and herding dog protectiveness. Both qualities are strong in Collies and both come in useful at different times. Only the Collie seems to know when one or the other is appropriate.

Penny had the run of the house, being Carol's girl, while Bully and Lance secured the outdoors. They had free reign of the well-fenced Sunrise Acres so that they could check on the safety and whereabouts of all of the farm's inhabitants.

Even though they were only a few months old, these two male Collies were already feeling their herding instincts begin to well up inside them and would keep close watch on all of the chickens, horses, goats and other new inhabitants. After all, if you are a Collie, and there are goats, chickens and other livestock around, how can you not herd them, control them and otherwise keep them in check? It's simply in your blood. And so it was, with the Collies of Sunrise Acres as the Acres began to grow into a successful working farm under Carol and Mark's management.

Neighbors had commented on the attractive trio of Collies and asked the human inhabitants if they had any plans to breed them. Other farm owners in the region had similar needs for a good, working dog that could also help with snake and varmint control. It was ancient Scotland all over again.

Carol had begun talking with Mr. Billingston about the possibilities of breeding the Collies they had bought nearly a year ago. Michael began gradually sharing with Carol what his years of experience with this wonderful breed had taught him. He tutored her as a master tradesman would tutor and mentor an apprentice. Carol had a knack for raising animals and had previously begun breeding and selling rabbits, guinea pigs and a few smaller breeds of dogs. Their stable of horses had begun to increase in numbers, and their chickens and goats were on the increase as well.

She had started a web site to advertise various animals for sale, and word of mouth soon spread that Sunrise Acres was becoming a burgeoning breeding farm for animals of all types. But, of all the animals that Carol had rapidly picked up and successfully started breeding, the Collie was different. Collies were more complex and mysterious. There was real history behind this noble breed, and Carol soon learned that breeding Collies successfully was not simply a matter of putting the would-be parents together and waiting for the offspring. So began Carol's quest to breed the perfect Collie.

Kevin L. Brett

Chapter 2
The Perfect Christmas Gift

Keith had convinced Linda that the Collie was the perfect dog. They also decided that it would make the perfect Christmas gift.

"That's going to be such an awesome gift for the kids," pondered Keith aloud. "I can't wait to see their reactions when they first see the little guy. What could be better than to receive a new adorable puppy for

Christmas?" Keith finished. What could be better than that puppy being a completely wonderful, loveable Collie?

"I know. I'm still worried about all that hair though," said Linda.

Linda would most likely be the one to vacuum up the hair and to give the little growing fur ball frequent brushings in an attempt to control the relentless shedding. Keith, now sounding like one of the children himself, "I'll make sure to walk the dog and take care of it when the kids stop," he assured. "And, I'll help groom him as often as needed, to keep the hair under control."

How could Linda argue? It was quite clear from Keith's pleading, that he wanted the dog as badly as the kids did. In fact, Keith was feeling like a child again, thinking back fondly to the many enjoyable times with Macintosh and Lad and starting again, after many years, to feel that child-like excitement of having a giant, furry, loveable Collie. Collies typically have sweet dispositions that are simply hard to resist, and they are very affectionate and caring companions. Linda thought to herself that she could see the future just a little bit more clearly than Keith could. Nonetheless, the Barnes family was already on a non-stop course with destiny, and an adorable, furry little Collie package was soon to become part of the picture.

The next question was where to buy a Collie. The first possibility in Keith's mind was to contact the original Piney Branch Kennels where his parents had purchased Lad those many years before. Lad had been the pick of the litter, and it was hoped that he would have been a show Collie, but as he grew, he developed a very slight fault. A fault is something that, in the show dog world, is a showstopper. In dog shows, there are different features that a dog of a certain breed must follow, known as the standard. The standard governs such features as their coat characteristics, overall body proportions and the shape of their face, muzzle, head and torso. If a dog competing in the ring does not have the proper shape, proportions, or other required features, they can be disqualified and will not have the opportunity to compete widely, if at all. Unfortunately, the fault that Lad had developed was the shape of the base of his skull. It was not visible to the eye, but to an experienced judge in a dog competition, it was as visible as the muzzle on the dog's face. A judge would run his hand over the dog, feel the shape of the Collie's skull and discover this showstopper. Lad would never be shown in competition.

In every other way, Lad was a beautiful and magnificent Collie, with an impressive pedigree. His father had been a champion, and he was Collie of the year on the national level. Keith and Linda did not want a show dog, but were simply hoping to find a very good quality Collie that was well bred, with a healthy lineage.

Keith looked on the internet for information about Piney Branch Kennels and found a listing with a phone number. He called the number, anxious to revisit the Kennel where his parents had taken the family one remarkable day to pick up Lad. Now Keith was excited to do the same for his family. Unfortunately, when he spoke with the person at the other end of the phone line, he found out that the Piney Branch Kennels were no longer breeding. The owners had retired a number of years earlier after several decades of successful breeding and showing. They were not familiar with any current breeders in the region, so they could not provide a reference to continue their search.

Keith and Linda began to search listings of Collie breeders on the internet. They looked for affiliations and registration with leading dog organizations as some mark of quality or legitimacy. Linda found several breeders who looked promising and called each of them. Finally, she narrowed it down to two in Central Virginia. She called to see if they had any Collie pups for sale. One had just recently sold the last of their most recent litter, but the other breeder at Sunrise Acres had some sable and white Collies from a recent litter and was expecting another mixed litter soon.

"If we buy one from the current litter, they would be ready way too soon. We need to get one from a litter that will be closer to Christmas," commented Linda.

"I think the timing of the second litter would be perfect," noted Linda. "The breeder assured me that the Collies were carefully bred. She seemed pretty knowledgeable and honest. She said none of them had

Collie-eye or any other common medical or genetic issues in their lineage."

Collie-eye was one of those peculiar medical conditions, toward which some lines of Collies were more predisposed. More than fifty years ago, this ailment had been identified, and at the time, it affected more than ninety-percent of all Collies. Today, with careful breeding, the number of Collies affected has been greatly reduced.

Sunrise Acres had inherited three Collies with perfect eyes and no other medical issues. All Collie pups were guaranteed to be free of all major medical issues. Hip dysplasia is another evil that can befall a Collie, causing serious hip issues, pain and immobility. Hip dysplasia is a condition, in its worst forms, which motivates many owners of these poor canines to have them put down. While some breeders suggest that crating a dog during his or her first year can cause hip dysplasia, there is no evidence to support that claim. It is genetic, but fortunately very rare in Collies.

Linda called and spoke with Carol. "I told her about the kids and what type of yard we have and that we were looking for a good quality Collie as a family dog, not for show," Linda recounted to Keith. "I was nervous and not totally sure what questions to ask," she confided. Linda was starting to feel a childlike excitement as the prospect of dog ownership grew closer. Linda's parents had a wonderful Cocker Spaniel named Lady, whom she adored, but Lady had recently passed away after fourteen fun-filled years. Linda was now looking forward to having a new fury bundle of joy scampering around the house. She was really looking forward to seeing her girls and son playing and growing up with the newest member of the family. Thinking back to her childhood dog Zeus, the line from the Lassie movie echoed in her ears. It was true; dogs just help kids grow up right. They have a pretty wondrous effect on parents too!

Linda had emailed Carol with a few follow-up questions later in the day after her initial phone conversation. She was nervous, excited and practically beside herself. She did not want to make a poor choice.

"What if something ends up being wrong with the dog after we bring him home?" she asked Keith, nervously. "What if he has some unforeseen ailment or condition that no one had predicted or detected? I would just hate to see something happen, where he was unable to be the ideal pet and play with the kids, or worse. What if something really bad developed and he had to be put to sleep? It's just making me sick!" worried Linda.

"It'll be ok babe. Quit worrying so much. Focus on the exciting side. We're getting a Collie," assured Keith. Linda's imagination was running amok. "It seems to me that you've discovered a really good breeder, who not only knows the breed, but she's gone to great lengths to make sure they are really good dogs." said Keith.

Linda, like any expecting parent, was anxious and wanted everything to be perfect. She wanted a storybook beginning, middle and ending. It wasn't that she couldn't deal with imperfection, or issues, or problems, she just didn't want the children to have any negative experiences with a new pet. She didn't want the children to be disappointed. Who would want a childhood memory of a poor disadvantaged puppy suffering his way through life and dashing all those dreams and hopes of this idyllic canine companion growing up in the Barnes idyllic neighborhood, in their idyllic house? How ridiculous! That wasn't the type of person Linda even was. She was not into image or keeping up appearances. She just wanted everything to be ok for their first experience with a family dog. She wanted her children to have the same kind of happy memories that she and Keith had experienced with their dogs. She just needed to get the butterflies out of her stomach.

Back came the reply from Carol. Linda was up early the next morning, checking her email to see if there was any word; some consolation for her concerns; some ease of her increasingly fretful conscience; just something from Carol that would put her mind at rest and assure her that everything would be fine, and Carol did. She assured Linda, that after many litters, they had never had problems with any of their Collies. She took the time to explain how over-breeding could result in very nervous and almost neurotic dogs. Carol explained how the dogs were checked by a board-certified ophthalmologist for Collie eye, and how her vets checked for a host of medical conditions and performed a battery of genetic tests to ensure the highest quality product; the perfect Collie; the perfect Christmas gift.

"Shew! That email arrived just in the nick of time - what relief!" said Linda to Keith as she finished reading the email. What a sense of unnecessary worry and stress she thought. "I guess everything will be ok after all," said Linda.

"I told you," chided Keith. "Carol said it would be. You can trust her. She and I go way back," Keith joked. She did indeed make Linda feel at ease and allayed her concerns.

"I feel better now. I just needed my questions answered," said Linda. She began to feel a wave of relief wash over her. "My goodness. All this about a dog!" she said looking at Keith as though she couldn't believe how worked up she had gotten.

"Hey. It's not just a dog. It's a Collie," retorted Keith with mock indignation and a smile.

Finally, the day arrived. Penny was ready. Carol and her breeder assistants were ready. The vet was on hand. Mark had even taken off the day from school, sensing that the time was right. His normal fall curriculum, introducing the principles of particle physics to his high school seniors, would have to wait a day. He had a little particle physics of his own to attend to today. Penny was breathing heavily, and a completely new litter of Collie pups was soon to be upon the Acres.

Then it happened, six perfectly tiny Collie pups appeared in rapid succession. Penny gladly gave up her burden, sighing now, not from the physical exertion of the event, but from relief. She had done her job, and now, as the vet inspected each Collie and placed it back nestled close to Penny, she began to nurse the tiny warm packages with her thick, nutritious mother's milk. These pups were starting their day off right, with a healthy instant breakfast drink and an ample measure of mother's love.

All of the pups looked wonderful and healthy. Everyone in the room was relieved to see that Penny was doing well and that the pups were all finding plenty of milk and snuggling close to mom. There was one small exception; in fact, small was the operative word. The litter was a mix of several blue merle Collies and tri-colors. One of the tri-colors was noticeably smaller than the rest of the litter; obviously the runt, but hey, they're always the more intelligent ones, or was it the more mischievous ones?

His runt status was quite evident as he wriggled and squirmed, eyes closed, next to his rather oversized sister, an abundantly healthy blue merle, nearly twice this little tri-color's size! Talk about a big sister. His immediate sibling was contently taking in Penny's milk, while this tiny runt was trying to find an opening to get in and acquire an equal share of the mother's bounty, or any share at all. Every litter must have a runt, and this little fellow was Penny's.

So began a many week process of feeding, cleaning, grooming and frequent vet checks, to ensure that all of the little Collies were primed, prepped, potty trained and photographed for the web site and positioned for selling to would be families. Carol was very particular, and she was concerned about making sure that her Collies were placed in what she considered good homes where they would be well cared-for and loved.

As much as Vicki and Sara enjoyed working for Carol with the animals and especially the wonderful Collie litters, they always had a strange, detached feeling about it. Here they would come to love the little fur bundles and spend many weeks caring for them; training and grooming them, and yet they could never refer to any of them by name, well because none of them had names. How strange it felt to be with a newborn creature that we typically think of by name when we buy or adopt a pet, and yet none of these perfectly adorable little guys and girls had a name they could claim. In fact, to make matters worse, in almost all cases, Vicki and Sara would never know any of their names. The prospective owners

45

would come to the Acres, as Mark liked to refer to it, and select a Collie. The financial transaction would ensue; the paperwork would be shuffled in the appropriate manner, and then the beautiful, fluffy, furry, cuddly little what's his name would disappear forever, and his or her name would never be known. The Collies were pets, with unknown names; going off into an unknown world to experience an unknown future with some unknown family. It was almost surreal, if you took the time to think about it.

The phone rang in Carol's kitchen just after nine-thirty in the morning.

"Hello Carol. It's Linda Barnes. How are you?"

"Hello Linda. I'm fine. What can I do for you?"

"I was calling to see how the puppies are doing. When do you think we could come by to see them?"

Carol explained the process and the particulars of the payment. She told her when the puppies would be available to take home. Linda was becoming more excited, this time, in a more positive way than before. She still had some concerns, a few more questions and just a touch of NNS – Nervous Nelly Syndrome. Carol did her best, again, to assure Linda.

"All of the puppies are doing great. They're all beautiful and healthy, and they've all been checked by the vet. None of them have any problems at all," assured Carol.

Linda was finally becoming convinced. Everything really was going to be fine. In fact, perfect. Things were going according to plan. The timing was working out great, and the puppies would be available to take home on December 20 just five days before Christmas. It would be a slightly early Christmas in the Barnes house. Who could hardly wait until the 25th anyway? That would be asking too much. The 20th was a Tuesday, so Linda and Keith would arrange to pick up the puppy that morning after taking the kids to school. They would take the Collie home and have him waiting to greet the kids when they came home from school. How perfect!

But, before this perfect plan could happen, they needed a dog. Keith and Linda first had to make their initial visit to the Acres to preview the litter and hopefully get there before too many of the litter were taken. They arranged to come and visit the litter one Saturday. They took the kids to Linda's parents, who only lived about twenty minutes away, then headed south to Sunrise Acres.

As Linda drove south on Interstate 95, Keith checked the map periodically, looking for the turnoff for Interstate 64 West which would take them southwest toward Sunrise Acres. Keith and Linda talked about how they would have to acclimate the children to the puppy and vice versa. They were concerned that the kids might become so overexcited that they might make the little puppy nervous or anxious. Now, all of a sudden, everything was centering on the possibility of having a new puppy and the Barnes family adjusting to the puppy instead of the puppy adjusting to the family. But, Keith and Linda were just excited. Zillions of thoughts were popping into their minds and bouncing off each other. They both felt like kids.

As they turned off the exit from 64 West to Route 522 South, which passed directly through Johnson's

Corner, Keith checked the map, for the thirty-eighth time. The countryside was beautiful, with an even mixture of small farms and forests. Johnson's Corner was not your typical one-stoplight kind of rural town – it actually had three stoplights running the length of the town. Here, Route 522 became known simply as Broad Street Road. Johnson's Corner was quite small, but still large enough to create that inviting, small town feeling. Almost everything one might ever need was right here. It was like a scene from the television show, Mayberry, RFD.

The directions said to continue southwest on Broad Street Road through town and take a left on Sully Road. Just at the outskirts was the Johnson's Corner Fire Department. About one-quarter mile past the fire department was the turn for Sully Road. Keith checked the map for the last time – the thirty-ninth. About one point three miles further should be the entrance to Sunrise Acres.

As the Barnes SUV cruised down the Oak-lined road, they spotted the sign that read Sunrise Acres Farm. They pulled onto the main driveway and headed down the two-hundred yard road toward the main house. The sides of the drive were lined with fencing, and as they drove along the road, there were several Collies running around and otherwise generally hanging out keeping a close eye on the unknown visitors.

Linda spotted a pair of blue merles and several sable and white Collies. Keith saw them as well. It brought back memories of that visit to Piney Branch Kennels when he was a boy. He reminisced about the kennels at Piney Branch. In his mind 's eye, he saw a golden-toned movie, shot in the warm afternoon sunlight with hazy edges as in a dream, filled with rich, honey-colored, sable and white Collies. As he admired the beautiful Collies, Keith thought to himself that a Collie kennel is just a simply wondrous place, permeated with a special kind of magic; a magic that could only be derived directly from the sunlight. At a Collie farm, the sun that shone down on the Collies surely had to have some mystical reaction upon contact with their coats, confirming in Keith's mind the source of the wondrous qualities of these dogs. Clearly, no other breed was endowed with the special magic of the Collie, of this, Keith was certain. His experience with Collies since childhood convinced him so.

What a grand sight. There were at least six mature Collies that Keith and Linda spotted scattered about the property and three younger ones that appeared to be about six to eight months old. They were lying beneath some very large Oak trees enjoying a cool morning breeze. Their thick fur coats made Keith think of a pride of lions basking in the shade on a hot afternoon on the African Savannah.

Linda pulled the SUV over to a small parking area on the front side of the white farmhouse. They got out and looked all around, taking in the scene. The Collies came walking cautiously up to Keith and Linda to check out the visitors. The apparent leader of the pack of Collies barked two loud announcing barks toward the main house, notifying Carol that visitors had arrived. Keith and Linda were under close scrutiny by three very capable Collies. While the Collies, by nature, are very friendly, none of Keith and Linda's movements went unnoticed by these watchful guardians. The Barnes thought the Collies were being cordial and friendly, but being the good shepherds that they are, these wolf-descendents were actually keeping the Barnes safely in check as they waited for Carol and Mark. Although Keith and Linda might not have felt it, they were nonetheless, surrounded. The Collies escorted them as they slowly walked toward the house.

Carol came out after hearing the announcement from the lead Collie. She walked out on to the front porch.

"Hello Mrs. Barnes!" she called from the porch. "Come on up. Don't mind the security detail. They're just greeting you."

Linda stepped forward, anxious to meet Carol. With just the few phone calls and emails that she had exchanged with her, Linda felt a bond with Carol. Women did that kind of thing. Keith followed Linda up the steps of the front porch and headed inside the small one-story house.

The farmhouse had a small, front living room to the left of the front door and a cozy library office to the right.

"Please excuse me a moment while I go get one of the girls to bring out the pups. I'll be right back," said Carol.

While the Barnes waited, they could see a small penned in area in the rather large kitchen, directly back from the short, hallway that lead away from the front door. It had a litter of Golden Retrievers, nestled in a bed of cedar chips in a soft round fleece bed. The Barnes enjoyed watching them for a few minutes, realizing that all puppies are quite simply, adorable and lovable. Then Carol and two assistants walked out with a Collie pup in each arm. There were six furry, lovable pups; two blue merles and four tri-colors. Keith and Linda were amazed at these six tiny fur balls. Their coats were so fluffy and thick compared to the litter of retrievers. These little fellows were clearly bred for a very different type of climate.

One of the blue merles was significantly larger than any of the other Collies. It was a female, with a beautiful, blue-grey coat, with the trademark black patches of a blue merle. The appearance of the coat reminded Linda of the look of dappled sunlight on a walkway in the summer time. The other blue merle was about the same size as the four tri-colors. Although they both found the blue merles beautiful, Keith and Linda gravitated toward the tri-colors. Their striking jet-black coats with brilliant white ruffs and rich sable facial markings and sable edging around the insides of their legs produced a striking appearance.

Carol and her helpers placed the puppies down on the moderately slick, wood floor. Keith and Linda immediately sat down on the floor to be with the pups. Linda began petting one of them and watching how it interacted with her. Keith was busy with two tri-colors of his own. Linda was making one of them run around in circles chasing after her finger. Her Collie was alert, but when she held him, he acted very nervous and hyper and did not seem to enjoy being held. She played with him a little and then moved to one of the others. Keith had found one of the tri-colors, who seemed to be very alert, but was also quite playful. When Keith tried the same thing with his finger as Linda had done, this little tri-color made a subtle purring sound.

"Look Linda. He's showing his stuff!" Keith laughed.

"That's not a purr. That's a growl!" said Linda jokingly. Keith reached out to pet the little fellow. He ran his hand along the Collie's back and felt his tiny, bony frame below the thick fur. Keith was playing keep away with his finger and felt the Collie's body vibrate as he uttered another of his fierce "growls". When Keith held him in his lap, he rolled on his back comfortably and exposed his tummy as he continued to try to nibble on Keith's finger with his minute little needle-like baby teeth.

His belly was covered partially with white fur, but there was ample pink puppy skin visible, and Keith gently rubbed this little guy's underside. The Collie seemed quite content to continue playing with Keith's finger as he lay on his back enjoying his comfortable perch in Keith's lap. Keith really liked the fact that this tri-color seemed, alert, but calm and playful and comfortable when being held by him. Keith had a good feeling about this pup.

Keith pointed out this little one to Linda as he put him down on the somewhat slippery wood floor. He continued to play and roughhouse, slipping on the wood floor. He scrambled around on the floor, slipped sideways and crashed in a tiny thump of fur. He immediately wrenched his tiny little body from lying on his side and pulled his legs underneath him quickly in a sudden flip. Instantly he was upright. He stood up again ready for another daredevil run at that circling finger. Linda was enthralled with this little furry wonder. He was so happy and supremely playful. He was quite content, laying in Linda's lap comfortably chilling out or continuing to burry his sharp little baby canines in her finger.

"Keith, I think this is the one," declared Linda.

"Yep. I agree. He seems really alert and playful, but he's able to be calm as well," commented Keith.

They decided to take this puppy. He was purfect. Keith and Linda made their down payment to Carol and Mark; took a few pictures for the scrapbook and walked back out of the farmhouse to their vehicle. As they walked toward their SUV, Keith had to walk along toward the area under the shade trees where some of the other Collies were arrayed. He knelt down so as not to seem like a threat to these guardians. While they are beautiful and appear almost too pretty to be a threat to anyone, the Collie is as well armed, well protected, and vicious in a fight as any wolf, but will only fight if forced. Keith did not pose any threat, and the Collies sensed his friendly manner, allowing him to pet them and talk to them for a few minutes before leaving.

Linda looked on as she stood by the car. Keith seem swallowed up in a sea of fur, from Collies all wanting to be around this friendly visitor. Keith was savoring this moment, as he tried to imagine a little ways into the future when the Barnes home would have a larger version of one of these wonderful dogs. Soon, the Barnes children, Keith and Linda would all have a new chum.

On the ride back to Stafford, Keith and Linda discussed possible names.

"What will we call him?" asked Linda.

"There has to be a Scottish name in there somewhere," stated Keith.

"Why?" asked Linda.

"Because he's a Collie," said Keith, almost surprised that Linda would ask such a question. "It's a Scottish breed. You just have to have a Scottish name in there somewhere. Ya cannough hef a Collie wi-out a Scottish nem!" he scowled, in a mock Scottish accent. "It's sacrilegious not to," he said sarcastically. "Besides, my previous Collies had Scottish names – Laddie and Macintosh," he reminded her. "Can't get much more

Scottish than that," finished Keith. "So we have to find him a Scottish name. Am I getting through to you? What part of Scottish are you not picking up on?" Keith joked.

"Ok. I think we've established the fact that it has to be a Scottish name," agreed Linda. "So, how do we know, which names are Scottish?"

"My dear wife, have you not heard of this wondrous thing called the internet?" suggested Keith.

"Smart alec," retorted Linda. "I don't suppose you have a Scottish internet to look at?" she jested.

"I might," said Keith.

That evening after the children were in bed, Keith and Linda searched the internet, the regular one, and found several name sites with Scottish names. They wanted to know the meaning of the names as well.

"I don't just want to pick a name though. I want it to be a name that fits the personality of the dog," requested Linda.

"I know. We'll find something that's just right," assured Keith.

But, what was the personality of this little fur ball? The pure black color of his fur made Keith think of a pirate, and his personality was somewhat comical and devious, but very lovable. Keith thought that it would be fun to name the dog Captain Jack, after the movie character. Given his personality, and the fact that he was black and mischievous, the name seemed like a perfect fit for this Collie.

"Linda, what about Captain Jack. After the character in that pirate movie the kids love?" inquired Keith. "He's black, like a pirate, and playful and rascally," continued Keith. "You know the kids would love that."

"The kids?" she said, with a deadpan sarcastic, wifely look, knowing that Keith was excited about naming the little guy.

"I don't know. I have to think about it some," considered Linda.

"Oh, c'mon, let's have a fun name," implored Keith.

"Is Jack a Scottish name?" checked Linda.

Looking up Jack on the internet name sites, Keith confirmed that, in fact, Jack was a name of Scottish origin.

"Look Linda," as Keith pulled up a web site with name meanings. "According to these web sites, Jack is of Scottish origin and means – mischievous and fun-loving. That sure seems to fit this little guy," concluded Keith. "What do you think? I think it would be really cute and fun to call him Captain Jack," pleaded Keith.

"That would be a lot of fun," decided Linda. Jack sounds fun she thought, as she visualized everyone calling him here and there.

"And, here's another important point. Collie names are often short, one or two syllable names, because when a shepherd has to call his Collie from a distance it is easier to hear a short name like Jack, than some longer name that might get lost in the wind," offered Keith.

"Of course, because he's going to be herding so many sheep on the mountainside," she joked.

She pondered it for a moment and then agreed with Keith. Captain Jack it was. That would be fun for the kids.

It was Scottish. It seemed to fit his personality, as far as they knew it, and it was a cute name.

"So, let's call him Captain Jack," suggested Keith.

"Alright," agreed Linda. It was settled. Captain Jack would be coming home to Stafford in a few weeks.

Chapter 3
A Pirate at Heart

The pickup day had arrived. It was December 20, and the children would be at school when their special Christmas package arrived home. Keith and Linda had already gone to the nearby pet store to buy a few essentials for their new puppy; a soft fleece bed, a potty training tray to go near the back door, a bag of cedar chips to get him used to going in the tray, as the breeder had trained him to do, a food bowl and a one-gallon self-filling water bowl. Of course, they had to pick out a leash and collar as well. They had already purchased puppy food, training treats and a few toys. It was almost as complicated as when they were buying all of the essential items for the children when they were expecting them to be born! Keith was determined he would have the little fellow trained in nothing flat. He also bought a couple of dog training books to help in that effort.

They headed south again on Interstate 95, following the route to Johnson's Corner. Soon, they were pulling into the long driveway leading toward the farmhouse. Keith looked out the window at the Collies as they trotted to catch up with the Barnes's SUV once again. He saw the same familiar troop of Collies from their first visit. As their vehicle came to a stop, Keith stepped out and knelt down to greet the furry, canine keepers of Sunrise Acres.

Keith and Linda met up with Carol at the front porch.

"Hello Carol," greeted Linda.

"Hello there," called Carol from the front porch.

Linda, Keith and Carol exchanged pleasantries, while Carol's husband Mark went to get the Barnes's new Collie.

Mark came back a moment later with Jack. He was adorable and much larger than before. He was very alert, looking right at Linda as Mark handed him to her. Keith gleamed excitedly as he looked on at their new family member. His paws were snow white, and they looked so pure in contrast to his black torso and the black upper parts of his front legs. He had an equally white ruff, a white tipped tail, sable muzzle, two sable-colored patches above the eyes and sable on the forward edges of his rear legs. He was beautiful.

He had striking markings, combined with his bright, inquisitive little face, very alert eyes and a miniature, wet, black nose. Although, oddly, Collie's eyes are typically almond-shaped, this little guy's eyes were round. Regardless, what an adorable package, thought Keith. The kids would be absolutely thrilled.

Carol began to finalize the paperwork, and Linda made the final payments. Mark took Jack back for a moment and inserted an electronic identification computer chip under his skin, between his shoulder blades. He tested it with a scanner, to make sure it was functioning properly, and Jack was all set!

"Carol. Thank you so much for all your help," offered Linda.

"Oh, no problem, it was my pleasure. We just love to see when these little guys get settled into a good home, and from what you have told me about your past experiences with Collies, I think he will have a wonderful home and family," assured Carol.

"We're so are excited to get him home and surprise the kids," said Linda. Turning to Keith, "I guess we'd better get going so we can be home before they do," she pointed out.

And with that, all of them walked outside toward the Barnes's SUV. Keith had put the little padded dog bed in the back seat so Jack could lay in it on the way home. Keith would sit in the back seat with Jack while

Linda drove. The troop of Collies came around as the party of humans walked out of the house. The lead Collie, whose name turned out to be Lance, barked several times, almost as if asking what Keith thought he was doing taking one of his pack with him. Keith knelt down and allowed Jack and Lance to rub noses for a moment. Lance gave Jack a couple of friendly nudges and one big uppercut swipe of his large tongue, as if to give him an officially sanctioned send-off, wishing him all the best. Keith petted Lance on the head as Lance nuzzled up to his hand. He stood up and climbed into the back seat with Jack.

Now that the dogs had said their goodbyes, it was ok for Carol and Mark to send off Keith and Linda. They buckled in and turned around to head down the driveway toward Johnson's Corner and the route home. For a while, Jack climbed up on Keith's chest and leaned forward on his right arm, trying to get a view out the window, of the passing scenery. Keith just held him there, with his right palm, supporting Jack's back so that he would not fall or suddenly try to wriggle loose.

After a while, Jack was content to be placed down in the soft fleece bed. He immediately wiggled forward, toward one of the three inch tall, padded sidewalls of the bed enclosure; nuzzled his nose against the soft fleece and closed his eyes. He looked completely carefree; completely adorable, and completely Collie-like, thought Keith. A few moments later, Jack practically fell on his side and completely flaked out. He slept for quite some time as Linda drove the SUV home.

"Are you interested in some iced coffee babe?" asked Linda.

"Sure. That sounds good," replied Keith.

"I think we're coming up on a truck stop pretty soon," as she continued north on Interstate 64. "It would probably be a good idea to let Jack out on his leash to see if he needs to do any business," she added.

A few miles later, Linda pulled their vehicle off the highway into the truck stop. The change in speed and feel of the car made Jack lift his head and start to look around. Linda pulled into the parking lot and found a spot over near a grassy area. Keith and Linda got out of the vehicle with the tiny black and white fur ball.

Keith put Jack down on the grass and let out the leash. The grass was newly cut, but was still standing up a good four inches tall. To Jack, this was practically like running through the jungle. His short little legs did their best to try to find sure footing amidst the thick grass that reached almost halfway up his chest. He tried to run and bound around a little, but it was simply too thick. He soon stopped; just trying to walk without falling down, which he did several times.

Suddenly, Jack froze; he raised his muzzle into the air and sniffed briefly, trying to identify a scent that he had never encountered. He began to generate his miniscule, but ferocious purr-like growl. He had spotted some birds picking through the grass. He immediately headed toward them, but what Keith had not noticed was that directly in the path between Jack and the birds was a turtle. There in the middle of the grass, at the edge of some woods, beside the parking lot, was a good-sized, nine-inch long turtle. Keith recognized the markings and overall appearance as a snapping turtle. Jack had smelled the turtle, and it was the turtle's scent, not that of the birds, that had caught his attention. The turtle was about sixteen inches away from Jack, either oblivious, or completely un-intimidated by this miniature wolf descendant. Perhaps this was a biker-turtle with an attitude! The turtle didn't seem to care. The turtle was not apprehensive about Jack, but Jack became quite excited about the turtle.

While Linda was inside the diner buying their coffee, Keith gave Jack just a little bit more leash to see how he would react once he got up closer to the reptile. The turtle and Jack stared at each other initially, but Jack was just too curious and kept making his occasional purr at him. The turtle turned and began to move off at an angle away from Jack. Jack would have no part of that. Mr. Turtle was going nowhere. Jack made two bounds; falling once, getting back up and catching up with the turtle. He immediately placed himself directly in the turtle's new path. The turtle stopped and stared at Jack. Jack just looked at him, as if to say, "Where do you think you're going buster?" Jack dropped the front half of his body and stretched his paws out in front in a low crouching position. Collies typically herd livestock by eyeing a sheep or other animal and maintaining firm eye contact to demonstrate that they are serious about keeping the livestock in check. The other technique these natural herders use is "slapping" the ground while in this low crouching position. Either of these techniques, alone, or in combination, is highly effective at keeping herds or flocks under control. These techniques also require the Collie to expend minimal energy to keep a large number of animals moving where he wants them.

It occurred to Keith, after watching this little clash of the titans unfold, that Jack was herding a turtle! They hadn't even gotten him home yet, and he was living up to his ancestor's traditions.

Linda pulled the SUV into the driveway. Once they were in the house, she went upstairs to her collection of ribbons and bows that she kept for gifts and found a red Christmas bow. She arranged it a little and brought a nametag down with it. Keith saw the bow and smiled, knowing that she was planning to put it on Jack so that the kids would see it when they arrived. It was 2:45 PM, and the Barnes's children normally arrived home from the bus stop at about 3:30 PM. Keith and Linda played around with Jack for a while and took him out into the back yard to do some more business.

Keith had placed cedar chips on the ground, in an area near the fence so that Jack would associate those cedar chips with the chips he had wet on in the training tray back at the farm. It actually worked, and Jack did his first business in the Barnes's back yard. What a glorious day this was! Everything was working out, so to speak.

"Here, let's put this bow on him. The kids will be home shortly," requested Linda. Keith held Jack toward her so she could attach the bow to Jack's collar. Once it was attached, she arranged it so that it lay just right. Then she took a pen, and on the gift tag, she wrote next to the "To:" label, "Sandra, Allie, Wes", and next to the

"From:" label, she wrote, "Mom and Dad", beside a small picture of a smiling Santa Claus.

Jack looked like something from a picture book. In fact, Linda grabbed the camera and took a couple of pictures of Jack on the floor and in Keith's hands. Keith switched with her and did the same with Linda and Jack. This was part of the unspoken understanding that Linda always wanted plenty of pictures of important family events and moments. Sometimes Keith had teased her that she had missed her calling, and that she should have been the White House photographer, or at least a photojournalist.

It was 3:32 PM, and finally, Keith, Linda and Jack heard the sound of the school bus pulling up to the bus stop about one hundred yards from the house. Keith heard the familiar screech of the brakes as the bus came to a stop. Linda decided to sit outside on the front steps to wait for the children, while Keith stayed inside, seated on the kitchen floor with Jack in his lap, waiting anxiously to see the kid's faces.

Several long moments passed as Keith sat with Jack. The tiny Collie was still, calm and soft in Keith's hands. Then, finally, the door opened as little Sandra walked in, her mouth wide open, followed by her older sister Allie, with the identical expression and finally by Wes, with a huge smile on his face and eyebrows raised so high on his forehead they practically touched his hairline.

"Oh my gosh!" gasped Allie. "It's a puppy!"

"Oh wow!" exclaimed Wes.

Sandra's expression shifted from an open gape to a sweet, excited smile. "Mama, Daddy, who's is it?" Sandra asked.

"Who's do you think it is?" tested Linda.

"Ours?" wondered Sandra.

"Yes it is sweetheart," replied Linda. "Merry Christmas guys," announced Linda to the three kids.

"He's ours?" inquired Allie, still in disbelief.

"Yes," confirmed Linda.

"Oh my gosh. I can't believe he's ours!" exclaimed Allie.

"He's so cute and fluffy," observed Wes.

"What's his name?" asked Sandra.

"Look at his name tag," said Keith.

"Captain Jack," read Wes.

The Barnes kids were so excited that they were beside themselves. They each took turns holding and playing with Jack, and all the while, Linda was, well, taking pictures for the scrapbook. Jack had instantly entered the hearts of the Barnes children, and Mom and Dad. Jack was home.

The first night was rough, both for Jack and for Linda and Keith. Jack cried, whimpered and pawed at the metal fencing of his enclosed sleeping area in the kitchen. Keith and Linda listened from upstairs in their bedroom and felt pity for the poor puppy.

"He must be lonely," worried Linda.

"He'll fall asleep in a little bit," assured Keith.

All parties made it through that first night ok. That was the routine for the first several days, until Jack started becoming accustomed to sleeping in his enclosure. As Jack became used to his new home and spent more time playing in the back yard, he began sleeping better at night. He had to know that he could whimper, but he would then simply have to go to sleep.

As he grew older, Jack's personality began to evolve and become more defined. Jack, like many Collies, was adorably mischievous. He was inquisitive, and excelled at immersing himself into everything he encountered. As Linda prepared dinner in the kitchen, Jack scampered around on the stone-tile floor, right around her feet, making safe walking a challenge. Eventually, Keith partitioned off the kitchen so that Jack was on one-half of the kitchen near the round, kitchen table while Linda prepared dinner in the other half of the kitchen.

Jack's fur became thicker and less fuzzy, almost the way a baby chick starts out with fluffy fuzz and begins to lose it as it grows. His coat had several interesting visual features. Normally a Collie has a ruff, which is the thick, white band of fur around his neck and chest. This fur provides natural protection, like armor, protecting the Collie's neck from potential attackers. On nearly all Collies, the white ruff wraps completely around the neck and connects to the large white area of fur on the Collie's chest; not so with Jack. His white ruff went from the right side, around toward the left, but just past his left ear, the white ruff stopped. There was a break in the white. From that point, around to the white fur on his chest, was black. Keith and Linda noticed this and thought it rather odd.

"Well, that is a very unusual marking," commented Keith.

"Does it make any difference?" wondered Linda.

"Not in the least," said Keith. "In fact, we'll call it his lucky break," he grinned to Linda. She smiled back.

Tri-color Collies also typically have a black face, with a muzzle that is sable on the sides, with an occasional touch of white. Jack was marked in that manner, but he had an adorably devious looking white streak that began between his eyes and went up his forehead.

"We could call that his wild streak," Linda declared jokingly. Jack had the look of trouble in his eye. He was adorable, fun and furry, but he was on a mission, even if he was not quite sure of the specifics of that mission, and with Jack involved, there was simply going to be trouble. Jack was already starting to live up to his pirate namesake's reputation of being lovable, but troublesome in a fun kind of way.

It was time for some personal hygiene, Collie style. Jack was in need of a bath, and Keith was up for the challenge; he thought. Keith prepared the bathroom. He had the dog shampoo, the towels and a special attachable showerhead with a hose that attached to the bathtub faucet. It was time to take the rapidly growing fur ball upstairs for his first bath. Keith picked up unsuspecting

Jack and carried him upstairs. Once in the bathroom, Keith placed the wiggling Jack into the tub and proceeded to fill it with warm water.

Jack slipped and wriggled, as he tried to figure out how to cope with this strange new sensation of the slippery wet tub. Like any puppy, Jack tried to find a way to climb out of the tub, in-between lapping up some of the water, as if the mere presence of the water reminded him that he might be thirsty. Keith proceeded to wash and rinse him. As he thoroughly rinsed Jack and soaked his fur, the previously fluffy hair began to conform to his tiny frame. He quickly took on the appearance of an oversized drowned rat. He was already small, but the water soaking through his fur made him look even smaller. Jack realized that his attempts to escape were futile, and he took on a look of surrender. Jack was a pitiful sight, and Linda made sure to catch multiple images of Jack's ordeal with her camera.

After the bath, it was time for the drying. Keith removed Jack from the tub and attempted to towel him down. Draping a towel that looked to be the size of a circus tent over the tiny Collie, Keith dried Jack, but toweling would only remove the water near the surface of his fur. With a thick-haired dog like a Collie, it's important to completely dry his fur down to the skin, but Keith knew he must be careful not to over dry his skin, or it would become flakey and itchy. Keith tried using a hair dryer set on low, but Jack would have no part of the warm air blowing over him, and the sound of the hair dryer was making Jack try to scamper around the floor of the bathroom. Eventually, after numerous tries, Keith was able to dry Jack's fur sufficiently so that he could brush it out into a fluffy mass.

Linda opened the dishwasher and began to unload it. Jack was sleeping in his fleece-lined bed when he heard the creak of the hinge on the dishwasher. He quickly lifted his head and looked around. In one quick bound, he was out of his bed. He came scampering, or possibly galloping on the slippery floor, around the corner of the kitchen peninsula to check out the strange sound. Linda smiled as Jack appeared around the corner. He stood for a second and looked at the strange contraption, as she slid the bottom dish tray out onto the grooves of the door so that she could access the lower level dishes. Jack came closer, cautiously sniffing and backing away occasionally. Finally, when he had worked up enough courage and confidence, he approached the edge of the dishwasher door. He lifted his paws up on the edge of the door and started sniffing the contents of the dishwasher. Linda grinned at the curious Collie and just watched him. She took in this precious moment and allowed Jack to experience the dishwasher, before having to make him go away. But, being the curious little pirate, Jack kept coming back. Finally, Linda had to put him in his enclosure, or there would be no hope of completing the task of unloading the dishwasher.

Kevin L. Brett

Chapter 4
Jack 101

It was time for serious business. Jack, being a highly intelligent Collie, had to begin to learn the basics, starting with, how to be, well, Jack. Keith had reviewed his dog training books; purchased an ample supply of training treats and several training clickers. He was ready. He put Jack on his leash and brought him outside to the back yard. He proceeded to give Jack his most important first lesson – his name.

Using the clicker method and treats is based on the theory behind the research and stories of Pavlov's dog. As the dog performs the desired action, the trainer clicks the clicker and immediately follows up with a training treat and praise. Each time the dog performs the desired action, the trainer emphasizes the name of the action so that the dog associates the name of the action with the reward of the treat. After the dog has adequately learned a new command, the trainer will only click the clicker and praise the dog occasionally. As the dog becomes used to the command, the trainer will not always offer the treat. The trainer will only skip the treat after the dog has become very responsive to the command over a long period of time. After enough training, the dog will learn to perform the command, with or without a treat or clicker, but periodic retraining with praise and treats is still helpful to reinforce the commands and keep the association fresh in the dog's mind.

In his first lesson, Jack was about to learn that he was, Jack. Keith had him on the leash and ignored him, while Jack played and sniffed every blade of grass. Keith walked to the end of the leash and waited until Jack was quite absorbed in the minutia of the grass in front of him. The little black, white and tan fur ball was quite busy and fascinated with everything in the grass. Then Keith called, "Jack!" When Jack looked at him, Keith clicked the clicker and immediately offered Jack a treat. Keith followed with "Good Jack." Keith moved away to the end of the leash and repeated these steps. After about seven repetitions, he was finished. Jack was now Jack.

Collies grow bored with too much repetition, whereas most other breeds will often perform the same trick or command endlessly. Collies simply will not. They learn quickly and require new stimulation. After a half dozen repetitions, Jack knew that he was Jack. How many times must one be called in order to prove that you know your name?

Later in the day, Keith brought Jack out to the back yard for a little repetition, just to be sure. "Jack," called Keith. Jack immediately turned his head, recognizing his name, and waited. Keith clicked and followed up with a treat; task accomplished. This drill was repeated two or three times daily, to reinforce Jack's recollection of his name while beginning to add other commands such as "Sit", "Stay", "Come" and so on. Jack made a great student and eagerly absorbed the new lessons, but only with about six repetitions of each.

Now it was time for Jack to move on to other important skills, such as how to notify his new owners that he needed to go outside to perform certain bodily functions. Carol and Mark had already trained the new litter of Collie pups to use the cedar chips in the potty tray. When the dogs went on the cedar chips, they would immediately take the dog outside to an area in the dog runs that had been coated with cedar chips. Keith and Linda continued that training method, and within two days, Jack learned to go outside and take care of important matters on the cedar chips. A few days after that, he knew to bark, such as his bark was. Keith also taught Jack to scratch at the back door to tell Keith and Linda that he wanted to go outside.

How does one teach a dog to scratch at the back door? Simple, by getting down at dog-level and scratching at the back door and then opening the door, and then repeating this process numerous times over a couple of days. That's all. After that, Jack got it. He knew how to ask to go out and how to come back in. Jack had mastered the goes-inzas and the goes-outzas of life. His IQ was rising daily. In less than two weeks, he had learned his name, a handful of basic commands and how and where to go take care of nature's business. Not bad, considering that he had only been on this earth for a few short weeks.

The Barnes back yard was a veritable jungle, if you were a two-month-old Collie. Jack reveled in his visits to this vast wilderness and always loved to romp around, roll in the grass and bound over the taller blades. There was a multitude of wildlife in the Barnes back yard, but Jack had not yet encountered all of it. As the days and weeks went on, Jack would meet up with skinks, snakes, rabbits, squirrels, birds and cats. All in turn, Jack would have a variety of wondrous and exciting experiences, with each of these strange new creatures.

He was now of the age that he really needed to be able to start running free in the back yard, but first Keith had to effect some minor modifications to better accommodate his new chum. Keith installed green wire mesh around the bottom of the fence all around the yard. With the fencing, Jack could not fit through the slats. Once the rabbit wire was installed, that would prevent Jack from crawling under the large shed, or under the deck that extended out from the rear of the house. Now Jack was free to roam, explore and grow.

Jack had experienced his first winter with the Barnes family and had enjoyed several romps in the snow each time there was a new snowfall in the Stafford area. Running through the snow at only three or four months of age, Jack had to struggle to navigate the six to eight inches of new powder. It required considerable effort to push forward and upward to achieve any forward movement at all in this dense white unknown matter.

The Barnes had inherited a beautiful log home from an uncle of Linda's who lived in Colorado. Keith was struggling with some financing, however, trying to determine how to handle some significant cost overruns on an addition that he was having built. This seemingly straightforward project was putting a considerable burden on their finances. Keith was investigating several options for regaining control of the project because he was simply running out of money.

While on a winter trip to their log home, Wes and the girls immensely enjoyed playing with Captain Jack in the snow and watching his reactions to it. He was delirious with excitement, experiencing a winter wonderland, as he bounded up and down through the seemingly endless expanse of white precipitation. His escapades resulted in a crisscrossing network of trails of small, Collie-sized impressions that traversed most of the yard. It was as if he sensed he was in his ancestral Scotland, bounding through the snow. He was perfectly at home in the cold, wintry weather; snow falling all around him; racing up and down his very own backyard highlands.

With Jack's thickening coat of fur, he was insulated from the cold, the snow and the wind. He could feel the press of the wind against his side, but he could not feel the bite of the cold, thanks to the thick protective fur that enveloped him. The only real contact he could experience with the snow, aside from the thick pads on the bottom of his feet, was to burrow his nose down in the snow. This he did numerous times with immense delight. He bored his nose down as deep as he could and lifted it up like an ice cream scooper, with a helping of cold glistening snow on top of his black, wet nose. Jack shook his head rapidly, rotating from side to side to fling the snow off; dive down for more and come up from his mining operation. Then he bounded off, creating more Collie impressions as he went. No one had taught him, and he had no example to follow, but somewhere in Jack's ancient DNA, was a bit of programming that told him that he could, or maybe that he should, just throw himself down into this amazing expanse of whiteness, roll over on his back and wriggle deliriously. Jack was making Collie versions of a snow angel! His facial expression and actions were pure mirthful excitement about his snowy environ.

At their Stafford, Virginia home, the steep hill in the back yard provided an outstanding locale for sledding, and the Barnes children had only to walk out the back door for a grand sledding experience. Watching Jack react to the winter snow was almost as much fun as partaking in the frolic with him. In fact, as Keith and Linda watched the festivities through the dining room bay window, it was hard to tell whether Jack was imitating the children playing in the snow, or whether they were imitating him.

Wes had conceived of an ideal new winter sport. It involved a sledding saucer, Wes and a certain wildly playful Collie, oh, and a hill. Wes grabbed his saucer sled and dragged it through the snow to the summit of the hill, placing it there on the launch pad. Then he marched down the hill, caught up with Jack and picked up the wiggling mass of excitement. Wes carried him to the top of the hill where the saucer waited. He sat down in the saucer and placed Jack comfortably in his lap. After making sure that the two new members of this "Olympic" sledding team were properly positioned and comfortable in their conveyance, Wes inched the sled forward, until it tipped over the top edge of the small, flat launching area atop the hill. Suddenly, the saucer accelerated rapidly down the hill; Wes holding on to Jack with one hand and the side of the saucer with the other. Wes let out a gleeful sound that was part laugh and part squealing yell. As Wes emitted his expression of delight, Jack supplied three forceful, but very adolescent sounding barks of approval, as if to announce that the duo was making tracks, and that all within earshot should take note.

Such exuberant and wildly joyful times were the stuff of Jack's puppy memories of his first winter. These adventures bounding across the snowfields of Jack's North Stafford, Virginia home would soon be displaced in his young Collie brain with new springtime experiences. The memories of this first winter would lay dormant in Jack's ever-expanding collection of new experiences, only to be re-kindled and experienced anew next year.

It was April now, and Jack was approaching six months of age. His coat was thickening, and the puppy fuzz that resembled the consistency of the fuzzy coat of a duckling was giving way to longer and slightly coarser hair. He was beginning to look like a small, lanky wolf, rather than a black and white ball of fuzz. Jacks legs were becoming long and slender, and his tail seemed almost disproportionately long for the rest of his body. As he stood, his torso was now much higher above the ground than just two short months ago. His longer legs now provided the essential lift to elevate him above the three-inch tall jungle of grass in the yard.

Other things about Jack were also changing rapidly. He was becoming more inquisitive and conscious of everything around him. His taller stature gave him greater mobility and ease of investigating whatever might happen to catch his eye or his scent. He was becoming more in tune to the inputs of his senses. While many dogs simply experience new sensations and aspects of their environment, Collies have a greater sense of mapping and making note of their environments and the inhabitants around them. Their herding and problem-solving instincts cause Collies to study, analyze and assess their environment and to keep their senses keenly tuned to potential trouble or issues that might require the attention of their higher cognitive skills.

Minding a herd of goats, or a flock of sheep, all day, by themselves, in the highlands, caused Collies to develop innate analytical skills and alertness that transcends the mere act of smelling, hearing and seeing. The Collie has developed a higher level of intelligence by interpreting his observations and sensory inputs to a greater degree than other domesticated breeds. They have learned to apply protective measures and developed tactics for managing large numbers of livestock, guiding them to pre-determined destinations for grazing, while avoiding areas where potential predators or environmental threats might await. They were required to manage their herds, keep them in safe areas and watch out for predators. These significant responsibilities required significant intelligence and independence.

All that fine discourse on intelligence aside, Jack was still a puppy, and as puppies go, he was still more than capable of behavior and other acts that would surely cause any observer to question this mighty canine intelligence. One could say that it is all just part of the learning process. At the same time that Jack's burgeoning intelligence made him capable of some levels of problem solving, this intelligence also gave him the ability to invent problems. Because of their intelligence and ability to learn quickly, Collies are also notoriously mischievous; just as intelligent children often can be quite mischievous; creating problems as a means of stimulation.

A thinking Collie has to be watched closely. Until a Collie has completely outgrown his puppy-like ways, by reaching an age of perhaps three or four years, it is necessary for the dog's owners to be vigilant and to constantly strive to second-guess the dog if they are to have any chance of preventing an endless string of unwanted acts. Two antidotes for this are ample stimulation and exercise. Without these, the Collie will seek his own entertainment out of sheer boredom. This entertainment can take many forms, not all of them entertaining!

Jack's bark was evolving. The kitten-like purr that Keith had first witnessed when he and Linda went to pick out Jack had developed into an actual growl and accompanying bark. Although the bark was still comparatively high-pitched and immature, it was nonetheless a bark, and it could carry through the air for a fair distance announcing Jack's presence. While his bark became approximately an octave deeper at age six months than it had been just a few short months ago, he was also developing various different types of barks.

Collies are known for chirping. When a Collie chirps, he makes a high-pitched and quite annoying bark to express boredom, dissatisfaction, or just a general need for attention. Jack had learned that if he wanted to go outside, he could use the old standby of scratching on the door, but in situations where the scratching was possibly out of earshot, he could augment his request with several loud and equally annoying chirps.

Jack was also discovering that there was a sizeable appendage extending outward from between his eyes. As his nose grew, he found it increasingly useful as both battering ram and probing device. He liked to walk past a low coffee table and repeatedly bat his nose at any books that might be neatly stacked, knocking them to the floor after repeated smacks. This minor act of mischief

probably had its roots in developing some useful skill
unbeknownst to the Barnes and probably to Jack as well.

Jack was growing and developing in many ways,
and every day added to his ever-expanding collection of
memories and experiences. In the years before Jack, the
Barnes had enjoyed landscaping their yard. Linda was
quite proud of her wide variety of plants and flowers all
around the grounds of their home. She enjoyed planting,
maintaining and caring for the many varieties of flowers
and decorative plants that adorned their home. She
enjoyed the beauty and variety of vegetation around their
home and felt a great sense of that maternal nurturing
instinct being satisfied by tending to her gardening.

In the back yard, a steep hill went up to a flat ridge
at the top. From the center of the yard, most of the way
over to the right side was a large, hillside oriental garden,
complete with pond and waterfall. During his first spring,

Jack had discovered that if he followed the path of small stepping-stones from the grass, up to the center of the island to the pond that he could stand at the edge of the pond and enjoy a nice drink on a warm spring day. It was cute the first time, and it was amusing the second and third time, but once this act became a routine, Linda was not at all pleased.

"Jack!" she exclaimed in frustration one day. "Get out of there! Go! Out!" she barked, as she clapped her hands together loudly, to try to startle him into leaving the island. He left, but not without leaving a mark, or rather several of them. He ran across a section of somewhat delicate ornamental grass, which was flowering. He trampled that and ran out and over the rock border that separated the island from the rest of the grassy portion of the yard. Jack left a trail through the trampled plants.

The next day was particularly beautiful and nearly cloudless with only a suggestion of a breeze. Jack had decided that the same soft bed of lush ornamental grass, growing around and underneath a beautiful, lime green miniature Japanese maple tree, would be the perfect spot to lie down and enjoy the shade. Linda was busy in the kitchen when she happened to look up and peer out the kitchen window. She had a perfect view of a young six-month-old Collie lying comfortably amidst the garden plants. Linda threw down her dishtowel and stormed around the large peninsula counter in the kitchen, out the back door, across the deck and down the stairs. All the while, Jack could hear the emphatic footsteps, and he could see her approaching rapidly. He sat blissfully, enjoying the shade and the comfortable padding of his garden bedding. He looked on happily, in complete comfort, delighted by the breeze as Linda walked up to him and swatted him on the bottom. Jack was completely startled. After all, he must have thought, what could be wrong with something so perfectly lovely and pleasurable?

He was supremely content. What could possibly be wrong with Linda? He jumped up, completely startled and taken aback by her stern admonishment. He bolted, yes, across the same stretch of landscaping he had traversed the day before. By now, under the weight of his four paws, and after several lightning fast journeys across this familiar piece of turf, Jack was forging a clear trail. This would become an ongoing battle between Jack and Linda until Jack finally determined, after several recurrences, that he would not suffer any further indignation. But, this battle over territorial rights was not completely over. Jack still had some final commentary on the matter.

A week or two later, after Jack had, for the most part, given up on the peaceful shade of the Japanese maple, he stood peering into the water at the edge of the pond. He looked up at the continuous flow of the waterfall, then back down at the ripples of water in the pond, and then he jumped. Jack went in feet first, all four of them. He splashed around, head above water and circled around in the small pond.

"Mom!!!," shrieked Allie, "Jack's in the pond!!!" Allie was completely startled and did not know how to react or what to think. For an instant, she worried about Jack drowning, but that concern quickly subsided once she saw him swimming about confidently, ears perked, looking quite content.

"Allie, what happened?" inquired Linda, as she came bounding down the steps of the deck.

"Jack was just standing near the pond. I thought he was going to take a drink, and instead, he jumped in!" she gasped, still hardly believing her own words.

"Help me get him out," ordered Linda. Linda and Allie approached Jack from opposite sides of the pond. It was like trying to lift up a small child out of a bathtub. Linda pulled him by the upper body, while Allie guided his back legs and set him down. He immediately shook himself off, spraying the girls with cold pond water. As they howled in frustration and part laughter, Jack took off and bolted across his favorite patch of plants in Linda's garden.

This time Keith became involved after hearing the commotion at the pond and listening to Linda and Allie's account of the event. Keith did not want pond hopping to become Jack's new pastime. He calmly walked out into the yard and called Jack to him. The unsuspecting Collie trotted happily up to Keith, with what amounted to a smile on his face. His ears were trimmed back flat against the side of his head in true Collie fashion, indicating that he was quite happy to see Keith. Since dogs essentially live in the present and simply do not remember their actions, even a few seconds after they have committed them, Jack did not even have the beginnings of a clue that Keith might be anything other than as excited to see Jack as Jack was to see him. Keith calmly picked Jack up and carried him over toward the pond. Keith knelt down beside the pond with his left arm wrapped around Jack's torso and proceeded to point Jack's nose down toward the water. Then Keith administered three very embarrassing swats on the lower portion of Jack's upper hind legs while simultaneously belting out three loud "No's" to accompany the three swats. Keith thought, it works with children; it should work with a supposedly smart dog. And so, that experience was registered in Jack's internal taboo list. Somehow, in Jack's intelligent canine brain, he implanted an association or a primitive memory that the pond was a source of unpleasant

sensations on his hindquarters, and that association with
the pond rose immediately to the highest level of Jack's
consciousness and quite possibly became a memory. Not
a memory of his jumping into the pond, but of the pain
associated with being near the pond, but that was enough.
That was Jack's last aquatic adventure in the Japanese
garden.

From that day forward, Jack only peered at the
water and watched as the frogs jumped back and forth in
the pond. Honestly wishing he could join them, but on
the other hand, content simply to watch the frogs enjoy
the water, while he maintained his station, avoiding any
further scorn or contempt from these overly demanding
humans. Jack was a pack animal, and he respected the
social obligations and hierarchy of the pack. To him, it
was clear that Keith was the leader of the pack; the alpha
dog. Jack just wished that maybe there was a less
embarrassing and distasteful way to be oriented to all the
rules of the home at one time, and not in such a
piecemeal manner.

The backyard of the Barnes home was practically a wildlife refuge from Jack's perspective. There were squirrels and birds of many varieties, with nests in many of the trees inside and outside the surrounding yard. There were field mice and skinks, which were like little lizards that scampered around in the corners of the yard and in and about the island. Jack delighted in trying to track the skinks down because they were so fast. There were turtles that made their way into the yard and headed in the general direction of the pond. Occasionally, one of the neighbor's cats came into the yard or walked along the top of the wooden fence; just to drive Jack insane.

On walks, Jack encountered other neighborhood dogs circling and sniffing each other using a customary canine investigatory technique passed down for millennia. Jack relished each of these new animal encounters, and each added to his sense of being part of a larger animal community. These experiences served to round out his understanding and appreciation of the wildlife community that surrounded him.

Kevin L. Brett

Linda was working in the back yard one Saturday afternoon, cutting back some of the tall, Japanese Silver Grass. Jack was keeping her company and just generally monitoring the yard for anything of note, as a sentry would monitor his territory. Linda was taking a bundle of the Silver Grass strands she had cut, over to the large trash bin around the front of the house. While she was gone, Jack decided to take a closer look at the area in the island where she had been working.

An unfamiliar scent drifted into his nostrils, carried by the slight movement of the air in the yard. It was the scent of some animal that he could not identify. He focused his senses closer to the Silver Grass, picking up a stronger scent. As he nosed in cautiously toward the base of one of the large plants, he smelled the scent quite clearly. He pushed aside a large amount of soft, fluffy fur and exposed a bed of more fur that was shaped into a nest. The nest was inhabited by four, recently born, bunnies.

They were not more than one week old. Jack continued to sniff and check them out. He gently nudged one of these strange furry creatures. Their eyes were still shut, and whenever he touched one of them, the baby rabbit jumped reflexively, like a miniature kangaroo.

Jack was fascinated by these quiet little bundles of fur. He kept nudging them curiously. Finally, he craned his neck forward into the nest and gently picked up one of the rabbits in his mouth. He sensed the helplessness of the infant rabbits and carried his find away from the nest and around the side of the house where Linda had gone. He walked up behind her and gently deposited the rabbit on the ground. Then he emitted two barks. Linda turned toward Jack and was surprised by what she saw.

"Jack, what it is?" she asked. "What have you got there big guy?" As if posing the question a different way would cause Jack actually to explain himself. "Oh my gosh, Jack, it's a baby. Baby what though?" she said to herself. "Oh, Jack, it's a baby rabbit. Where did it come from?" she continued, as she picked up the rabbit from the soft grass where Jack had laid it. "Let's go. Find the rabbits," she commanded. Jack barked twice more and took off toward the nest he had discovered.

Linda carried the solitary rabbit with her as Jack ran toward the nest. She approached the nest as Jack walked over and sat down beside it, then he bent down from where he sat and nosed the other rabbits one time, pointing to the nest with his nose.

"Oh, wow, look at you Jack. Look what you're found," she put the baby back in the nest. "Jack. Stay." Jack waited patiently, while Linda went inside and called the girls.

"Allie, Sandra. Come here," called Linda. A moment later, both girls came down the stairs.

"What mom?" inquired Allie curiously.

"Jack found a nest of baby rabbits. Come here, I want to show you," she requested.

"Ohhhh! Baby rabbits! How cute," squealed Allie with delight? Linda led the girls outside, where Jack was waiting. The trio headed over toward Jack, and as the girls came up to the nest, Linda lifted some of the overhanging Silver Grass so they could get a closer look.

"Jack found them after I cut away some of the extra plant stalks. When I went to throw some of the cuttings in the trash, he brought one of the rabbits to me in his mouth and laid it on the ground," explained Linda.

"Can we keep them?" pleaded Allie, instinctively.

"No sweetie. These are wild rabbits. I think something might have happened to their mother. They seem to be ok though," said Linda.

"But mom, we'll take good care of them. I promise," offered Allie.

"Girls, we have to take them to an animal shelter. Now, do me a favor and go in the garage and bring me one of those shoe boxes on the storage shelves near the gardening cart," requested Linda.

"We're going to have to take some of this fluff and put it in the box and then put the bunnies on top of that so they will still be in their nest," continued Linda.

"Ok," agreed Allie and Sandra in unison.

The girls headed off on their quest to find the right box to make a suitable container for moving the bunnies. When they came back, Linda used a small pair of garden shears and poked air holes in the lid and sides. Then she instructed the girls to scoop up an ample amount of fluff from the nest and place it inside the box. Once that was complete, she allowed the girls to carefully pick up the bunnies and place them in the box. The girls shrieked with excitement as the tiny bunnies jumped blindly. Their eyes were not even open, and they were jumping instinctively as if they were practicing for a few weeks from then when they would be ready to move around on their own.

"You are doing a very Girl Scout-like thing, girls. You're helping preserve nature and giving these rabbits a chance to survive," complimented Linda. Linda thought, what a perfect, real-life lesson in wildlife conservation. Linda and the girls hugged Jack, petted him and thanked him for finding the babies. They headed inside the house with Jack right at their heels.

Linda went to look up the phone number of the nearest animal rescue center while the girls were fascinated by peering into the box at the tiny, fury wonders wriggling around inside. Jack sat beside the kitchen table as the girls watched the rabbits. He barked twice more as if to say, "Don't forget, I'm the one who found them."

Linda located a woman who ran a local state licensed animal rescue center out of her home. She obtained the directions, and the woman said they were welcome to bring the rabbits out that afternoon.

"Girls, get the box and take it to the car. We're going to drive them over to the animal rescue center."

"Ok mom!" said Allie happily. They all walked toward the front door.

"Keith, Wes. Do you want to come with us to the animal rescue place?"

"Sure. Let's go Dad," retorted Wes eagerly. They were both interested in checking out the rescue center to see what kinds of animals might be there. Everyone headed out to the car. Keith was preparing to lock up the front door when Jack barked insistently several times at him. Keith understood that Jack fully expected to come along wherever they were taking his little friends.

"Come on Jack," commanded Keith. "I hear you found these little guys. Guess you have a right to see them off," he finished.

Like a happy little kid, Jack took off toward the front door and out to the car. He hopped in the back seat, and Wes let one of the split bench seats down so that Jack could climb into the rear area of the SUV.

"I guess the entire family is going along to see Jack's little bunny friends off to a safe home," observed Linda. "All right, off we go," she said as the Barnes SUV backed out of the driveway and headed down their street.

The encounters with the bunnies and all of the other forms of wildlife were just the beginning of Jack's ongoing series of escapades with many varieties of wild animals. There were five particular wild animals on the Barnes's property, to which Jack had taken a liking. Jack had his own wolf pack, in the form of the Barnes family.

Although, when he wanted any of the Barnes pack to go some place or move in a certain direction, he seemed to change his perspective on them from that of being his pack, to that of being his flock of sheep. In this regard, his herding instincts were becoming quite apparent to the Barnes.

One summer, Saturday afternoon, the Barnes had a couple of pallets of landscaping stones delivered to the house from the local nursery. Jack was on hand to greet and watch the men as they positioned the delivery truck to dump its load of stones at the edge of the Barnes property. Jack felt obliged to produce a consistent round of warning barks. These barks were not really the type that said, "You don't belong here and you are about to be eaten alive." They were more the garden variety, "Hey, I'm here. I see you. Keep it real. I'm a Collie."

Once the delivery truck had finished, the Barnes began busily loading the wheelbarrow with stones and trucking them to the back yard. Keith was the resident pack mule, and Wes and Sandra helped to load stones each time Keith brought the wheelbarrow back empty from depositing a load of stones in the back yard. Allie and Linda helped to unload the stones from the wheelbarrow rather than allow Keith just to dump them. They would all be smashed and broken otherwise.

As Keith pushed the wheelbarrow from the side gate around toward the back where the island and pond were located, Jack decided that Keith needed guiding. Every single trip that Keith made from the front yard to the back yard, Jack was there to nudge his legs with his nose and nip at his heels. Continuously Jack tried to close his entire mouth around whichever ankle was closest to him. Keith could scarcely take a step without Jack pushing or nipping.

Keith was being herded the entire time as if he was a runaway sheep who needed constant reinforcement about which way was the right direction. Once the last wheelbarrow of stones had been deposited in the back yard, Jack saw fit to escort Keith and Linda back and forth on virtually every trip from the rock pile to the garden retainer wall they were building. He waited until the stones had been laid in place and then accompanied

Keith, usually with a nudge or a nip at the heel, back to the rock pile, for the next armload of stones and back again to the stonewall. This ritual went on for a number of repetitions, until Keith had to have Jack sit and stay put and just watch without continuously nipping and nudging Keith or Linda all afternoon.

Earlier in the week, the entire family had taken Jack for a walk down the street and around the bend to a nearby park. Jack enjoyed these long walks immensely and always bolted out of the back yard at full speed with Keith in tow. He usually ran Keith until he had gone nearly halfway up the street, leaving the family to catch up later. Keith knew that this was not proper behavior to allow Jack the run of his leash, but since Jack was at this point, just a big kid who was excited to play, he allowed him to run off a little steam for the first one hundred yards of the walk.

The family made it to the park; the girls played on the playground, while Linda and Wes played catch with Wes's football. Meanwhile, Jack and Keith walked around the grounds of the park and ran back and forth chasing each other for fun. Linda recognized some neighbors who had also just arrived at the park. They talked as Linda played catch with Wes.

Keith was running Jack back and forth. At one point, he tried to walk Jack over to where Linda had stopped to visit with the neighbor. Keith and Jack proceeded to walk in that direction for a few paces when Keith noticed that Jack, walking on Keith's right side, began to nudge and push on his right leg. Keith continued to try to walk straight, in the direction of Linda. He was about thirty feet from his destination as Jack began to push even harder on Keith's right side. Keith started to turn in the direction Jack was pushing. Jack continued to push on Keith to guide him into a U-turn. Jack was turning Keith around forcefully, and once Keith had completed the U-turn, Jack slowed slightly so that he was just a pace behind Keith.

From his new position, Jack issued two very intentional pushes with his nose to the back of Keith's right knee. Keith allowed Jack to continue, just to see what he would do. After the two pushes to Keith's knee,

Jack then assumed his position alongside Keith and continued to walk straight, in the direction of their home. Jack had just herded Keith around in the direction he wanted him to go.

Linda called out to Keith, "Where are you going?"

Keith replied, "Apparently, Jack is herding me home. I'll see you later." Linda and her friend laughed. The girls and Wes grinned as well.

"Look, Mom. Jack is herding Dad! He thinks he's a sheep," exclaimed Allie.

Jack's herding instinct was like most Collies, instinctive and effective, and he used and practiced these skills whenever he saw fit. The Barnes children were quite amused with the idea that their Dad was being herded around by Jack.

Jack also had a habit of running around in the yard playing with the girls, coming up behind them and knocking them down. Unfortunately, when a ten month old Collie comes running at a good rate of speed and executes a body slam against a six or seven year old girl, the laws of physics demand that the young girl head

117

directly toward the ground at an equally good rate of speed.

Jack enjoyed running up behind the girls, purely in harmless play. He slammed them down to the ground, and invariably, whomever Jack had sacked would come up startled and usually in tears. Jack then proceeded to lick her face and nudge her upward with his nose. For a young girl to be hit from behind with the full force of Jack's playful mass was like being body-slammed by a "professional" wrestler and about as pleasant.

As Jack grew to be even larger and heavier than the girls, he fortunately developed a decent protective sense that maybe the idea of knocking these small girls down was something that did not bring as much pleasure to them as it did to him. He abandoned this practice in favor of simply jumping around them and licking their faces; something the girls relished certainly more than the unintentionally brutal assault of Jack's puppy-like football tackles. The girls appreciated this change in behavior. Jack had shown up on the scene at the Barnes home weighing a mere eight pounds. One year later, the girls had not increased significantly in size or weight, but Jack had grown to equal their weight in that very short span of time.

Most of Jack's other antics were very puppy-like and certainly not necessarily unique to Collies. Collies are known for being quite mischievous, largely due to their high intelligence and constant need for stimulation. In that spirit Jack was wont to grab any shoe he might happen to find lying around the house. Linda was a marathon runner and typically had several pairs of running shoes, training shoes and regular tennis shoes. She practically lived in them, but when she wasn't in them, she had a tendency to leave a pair somewhere in the house, and Jack took advantage of this opportunity.

Jack enjoyed a good, sweaty, smelly running shoe as much as any canine. He also simply enjoyed the chase. Whenever he picked up a shoe, he began to trot around the house in hopes that someone would notice that he had a valuable item clenched between his teeth. Once Linda or one of the others spotted him, they attempted to corner him in one of his favorite games. Often, Jack ran into the dinning room to the far end of the table near the bay window and stooped; looking down under the table to see from which direction his opponent was approaching. He enjoyed the back and forth, playing keep away with anything from a shoe to a sock, to one of the girls' hair bands. Anything worked, as long as it was something that he was not supposed to have and something that would initiate a chase. Once cornered, his opponent would belt out, "Jack! Drop it," and on command, he dropped the item and ran away; one point Jack, zero points opponent.

Jack also enjoyed chewing on bark and mulch in the back yard and any of the children's toys such as water guns. One afternoon, Keith was watering some new plants in the Japanese garden on the hillside in the back yard. Jack came walking around to where Keith was, to investigate this interesting device known as a garden hose nozzle. Keith had a pistol-shaped hose nozzle with a variety of settings to adjust the spray pattern of the water. He had it on a medium setting to drench the area around the new plants. Jack looked inquisitively at the hose and watched Keith for a few seconds, before deciding that he simply must conduct a more hands on, or mouth on, investigation into this strange device that was spewing liquid through the air.

Jack jumped at the stream of water each time Keith waved it in his general direction. Keith was simply waving his arm back and forth to cover the ground where he had been planting. Each time the hose came close; Jack jumped and snapped at the water. Keith left the hose just within Jack's reach to see what he would do. Jack stuck his snout right into the stream and began trying to lap up the water in the same manner as a child. He enjoyed not only the cool freshness of the water, but the startling and exciting stimulation from the intensity stream of water smacking him on the side of the nose and mouth.

It was springtime, and Jack and everything around him was growing, blooming and developing. Jack was simply the largest of the "things" in the Barnes area that were blooming. Like an awkward adolescent, he was growing faster than the amount of coordination that existed in his body at any given point in time. On too many occasions, he both accidentally and inadvertently knocked things around with his large nose.

Jack delighted in such minor annoying antics, just to push Keith and Linda's buttons. He knew exactly what he was doing. He knew he was not supposed to touch anything on the table, but what was the point of that? When someone picked a book up to give Jack a mock scolding for this latest violation of one of the innumerable laws of Barnesland, Jack often broke out with a sound that could not be described as anything other than singing. Keith or Linda would come up to Jack and wrap their arm around Jack's chest or torso, ruff up his fur, and hug him while continuing the mock scolding. Often, as they went through this ritual, Jack sang out in a very forlorn, pitiful tone, as if trying to evoke pity for his plight of having to give up his treasured shoe or other stolen item. This high-pitched combination of howl and crying serenade was a serious case of self-pity and woeful lamenting, Collie-style. It was completely entertaining for the Barnes and Jack relished the attention.

After such a scene, Jack typically retired to the cool, tile floor of the kitchen and leaned up against the butler's pantry cabinets off near the table. Almost inevitably, someone spotted Jack doing his best to survive the harsh living conditions that were his station in life, as he lay on his back with front paws extended fully upward and forward in the air and rear legs in similar fashion, belly-up.

Yes, this was a hard life for a Collie, and lying on his back, legs outstretched, was certainly an obvious sign of the tremendous stress that Jack endured on a daily basis, but he was glad to do it. Such hardship and dedication to duty were all part of the life of a Collie, and Jack was learning his responsibilities well. Overall, he was adjusting perfectly to the Barnes family and their home. He was blossoming into a beautiful Collie as he entered the spring of his life.

Kevin L. Brett

Chapter 5
A Thanksgiving Lesson

Linda was about giving. She had a very giving heart, and her upbringing and her faith had taught her three immutable principles for a successful and meaningful life:

Give of yourself, in time, talent and gifts.

Be thankful and appreciative for what you have, and you will find that you do not need as much as you think.

It is not so much what the problem is, but how you deal with it, that counts.

Her greatest aspiration for her children, was for them to come to know and practice these qualities and grow into giving, caring and compassionate adults. She wished for them an abiding trust in their faith that would provide them a wellspring of strength throughout their life. She wanted her children to understand that being sincere in their faith required greater strength of character and determination than to allow others to dissuade them from it.

Every day, Linda was tuned in for opportunities that might call to her where there might be a need to apply one or more of these virtues. Thanksgiving certainly fit the bill. Although Linda was thankful every day, for the many blessings in her life, Thanksgiving was the annual zenith of this attitude of gratitude and reflection.

Lately, the price of gasoline had been increasing dramatically, reaching record levels almost weekly. Keith and Linda both discussed the importance of not wasting resources. As Scout leaders, they both encouraged conservation with their children. There had been many recent news reports about record profits being experienced by OPEC countries and the major oil companies. At the same time, Linda noticed that, while OPEC nations were enjoying these record profits, the prices of basic food staples and other essentials were increasing correspondingly. To make matters worse, one particular oil rich country had decided that their annual contribution to the World Food Bank, which served impoverished and under-fed communities, would total up to exactly zero dollars.

To Linda and Keith, this was nothing short of abominable that a nation so wealthy would have a national culture so callous that they failed to sense any obligation to find some way to help or contribute to those less fortunate than themselves. Certainly, any modicum of national consciousness and social responsibility would dictate that all nations shared a collective responsibility to help improve the conditions of peoples on the brink of starvation and completely lacking the basics of life. Linda saw this attitude as a modern day manifestation of Scrooge from Dickens's Christmas Carol. Even the highly impoverished country of Bangladesh had pledged fifty-thousand dollars for food aid. Although the oil-rich kingdom in the Middle East was later shamed into parting with a contribution half the size of the one provided by the United States, in Linda's mind, the kingdom had already evinced their true sentiment to the world on the plight of their fellow man and those beyond their borders.

Recently, as a physical expression of their principles of service, Linda and Keith had involved the children in signing up through the World Vision charity. Through this organization, they sponsored a Muslim family in Ghana, Africa. Keith and Linda explained to their children the importance of sharing their blessings and good fortune with others who were struggling simply to provide the basics of life. Keith and Linda worked diligently at every opportunity to impress upon their children how fortunate they were to live in such a blessed country, neighborhood and family and how they were simply obligated, on many levels, to give back and help others, regardless of nationality, faith or ethnicity. This family in Africa simply needed their help and that was the only criteria. This attitude stood in stark contrast to that of the oil kingdom and their government. Through that country's example of reluctance to serve and help others, Allie, Sandra and Wes were learning important obligations that those more fortunate should recognize.

Certainly, the Barnes children felt very excited and fortunate to have Jack. Every day, the three children lavished numerous hugs on the more than accommodating Jack. They loved this wonderfully funny, mischievous Collie ever so much. In response to some of the hugs, Jack had developed a habit of walking between Keith and Linda's legs and pausing, just long enough for some rubbing and patting, ears pinned back, of course, in one of Jack's "smiles". However, a problem had begun to occur.

"Have you noticed Jack's right rear leg?" Linda said to Keith. "It seems to drag behind the other one sometimes," she continued. "Every once in a while, it almost looks like he has a slight limp on his right side. Why do you think that is?" she questioned Keith.

"I don't' know. I don't really see him doing any limping. I think he's probably just having difficulty with the slick floor," replied Keith.

"I don't think so. I've been watching him for a while now, and he seems to do it even when he is on the carpet," countered Linda. "I think he has some kind of kink in his hip, or it might be binding in some way," she postulated. Keith watched as Jack walked around, to try to notice any abnormality in his gait.

For the next several weeks, Keith and Linda kept a close watch, trying to determine if there was anything wrong with Jack, or if maybe, he was just having some kind of minor intermittent issue. Maybe he was just experiencing some form of canine growing pains. After close scrutiny over the course of many weeks, Keith and Linda were convinced that they needed to have Jack checked by the vet. They scheduled an appointment with Jack's vet at the Banfield Pet Hospital. The vet was located inside the Petsmart store on Route 610 in Stafford. Whenever Jack went to Petsmart for grooming, or to see the vet, everyone treated him like a local celebrity. Without fail, one of the groomers or the attendants at the pet hospital would comment to someone near them, "Look. There goes Captain Jack. Oh look, Captain Jack is back!" Everyone there was always glad to see Jack as if they were welcoming back an old friend.

The vet examined Jack closely and observed his gait. Next, she took a series of x-rays. When the results came back, she confirmed that Jack had hip dysplasia. Keith and Linda were stunned. She showed both of them the x-rays and explained that his right hip had seriously degenerated, and that his left hip had already begun to do the same.

"Wow," Keith commented to Linda, as they looked again at the x-ray after arriving back home. "You don't have to be a doctor to see that his right hip socket is all ground away and jagged," commented Keith, awestruck. "The vet said that this is a very painful condition, even though he does run around like nothing is bothering him," added Keith.

"Remember, he also said that Jack would be in a lot of pain over the next several years as he grows older, and that he would have a poor quality of life because of the decreasing mobility of the joint. She also said the pain would increase as he ages," added Linda.

Keith and Linda had asked the vet what options existed. She said that until just a few years ago, most owners would put the dog to sleep to prevent the pet from experiencing agonizing pain. She also informed the Barnes that in recent years, surgery had become a viable option. There were two possible procedures, either of which had the potential to eliminate the pain and provide nearly complete mobility to Jack's hip.

Unfortunately, the procedure was expensive, and it was likely that Jack would need the procedure repeated in a year or two for his left hip. Linda was in tears at the thought of Jack being in terrible pain. In her mind, the only choice was which surgical facility would perform the procedure. Neither of them was happy about the considerable expense, but both agreed that some things are more important than money and that they would come up with the money somehow.

"I can't believe the irony of the situation," reflected Linda in a frustrated voice. "Here we spent so much time searching for an outstanding breeder who assured us, in fact, guaranteed that the dogs were free of hip dysplasia and that there was no history of that condition in their bloodline," she continued. "I thought we had happened upon the perfect Collie when we chose Sunrise Acres and Jack," she said in a disbelieving tone.

That evening Keith and Linda had to explain to their children what was wrong with Jack and what they had decided to do about it. Linda also wanted the children to learn the lesson that was provided by this unexpected turn of events. It was a perfect convergence of three important truths. After dinner, Keith and Linda called the children into the family room for a family meeting. "Hey kids, Dad and I have some news we want to share with you," began Linda.

"What is it? Are we going to Disney World or Busch Gardens?" asked Allie excitedly.

"It's probably something lame, like we have to clean up our rooms," countered Sandra in her best four-year-old, sneering sarcastic tone.

"Stop it Sandra. You're such a loser," retorted Wes, attempting to quiet her down in his own completely ineffective manner.

"That went well," Linda sighed to Keith in her own adult sarcastic sneer, giving him one of those wifely looks of defeat and despair. "Guys, we want to talk to you about Jack," said Linda, trying to regain control of the conversation.

"What about him? Did he poop in the living room?" giggled Wes. "You should make the girls clean it up! They could be poopie cleaners! Loser, poopie cleaners," Wes offered, in typical antagonistic big brother style.

"Shut up Wes, you chicken head!" flew Allie's response to his affront.

"Guys, stop it! We have some really serious news about Jack, now behave – nicely that is, and listen," ordered Linda.

"Is he going to be ok?" asked Allie, starting to get concerned that something might be really wrong.

"Yes, he's going to be ok," assured Linda. "Come here," she motioned to Allie and Sandra. The girls came over to the oversized chair where Linda was seated and climbed up in her lap and snuggled close to her as she wrapped her arms around them, in preparation for her third attempt to get past the brother-sister pecking and antagonism.

"Jack has something wrong with his hip. It's causing him to limp and walk funny," she said. "But the important thing is that his hip is causing him to be in a lot of pain. Even though he runs around a lot, his hip is actually hurting him. Because he's still a puppy, he doesn't know enough to stop running," she elaborated. "Daddy and I took Jack to the vet today while you were at school. They took some x-rays of his back legs and hips. One of his back legs is grinding against his hip and its chewing up the bone and causing him a lot of pain," she said.

"Is Jack going to die?" asked Allie sadly.

"No sweetie," replied Keith. "But he's going to have to go to the dog hospital and have an operation to fix his hip," continued Keith.

"Can the doctors fix him?" wondered Wes.

"Yes," confirmed Linda. "But you know what guys. It's going to be very expensive for Jack to have this operation. Most people don't have the money to pay for a special operation like this for their dogs."

"What do they do?" asked Allie, with concern.

"Well," started Linda. "They make the dog comfortable and then they put him to sleep so that he won't be in pain anymore," she tried.

"You mean they kill the dog?" asked Allie getting really worried now and starting to tear up.

"Well. They let the dog go to sleep comfortably so that he isn't in pain anymore," repeated Linda. "But we're very fortunate because we're going to have him fixed up. So, he's going to be just fine."

"You guys aren't going to put him to sleep then?" worried Sandra.

"No, baby girl," said Keith reassuringly. "We're going to take him to a really good animal hospital that we've found. They fix hip problems like this all the time, and they're going to make Jack all better," he finished.

"That's right," reinforced Linda. "So there's nothing to worry about. We just wanted you guys to know what was going on with Jack. I also want you guys to be thankful and appreciate how fortunate we are that we're able to take care of Jack so that he will be healthy and with us for a long time," she finished.

"I think God gave us the money that we have that we can use it wisely and do good things with it like taking care of Jack. We're supposed to use our resources wisely, and I think God gave Jack to us because he knew we would take good care of him," observed Wes.

"I think you're right Wes, and Jack is very lucky to have us as his family because we are going to take good care of him," concluded Linda. "So, like we're always trying to teach you guys, we have to give of ourselves and help those who are in need right?" she queried.

"Right, and Jack needs our help to get better. So, we're going to help him out," replied Sandra.

"That's absolutely right Sandra," said Keith as he reached for Sandra and hugged her close.

Linda beamed as she took in the moment with her family. She was proud of her three children and special moments like this when they were able to pull together thoughts and sentiments that reflected the values and elements of faith that she and Keith worked diligently to impart to them. She was greatly concerned with consciously educating their children to develop the compassion and the predisposition for caring and giving and always being thankful for what gifts they have.

"So, guys, I think this is kind of appropriate that even though Jack is in pain, and his hip is bothering him, it is almost Thanksgiving and Jack's operation is actually going to be the day before Thanksgiving. We talked with the doctors, and we will be picking Jack up from the hospital and taking him home on Thanksgiving Day," said Linda. "So that's quite a Thanksgiving gift don't you think?" she asked.

"Yeah," replied Allie. "So Jack will have a really good Thanksgiving with our family, because we all love him so much, right?" she checked.

"You bet sweetie," affirmed Keith.

As planned, Jack had his surgery on Wednesday morning of Thanksgiving Eve. Linda took Jack to the animal hospital during the day while Keith was at work and the children were at school. Keith went to the hospital Thursday morning, Thanksgiving Day, to pick up Jack. When he arrived at the hospital, he was impressed with the way the interior of the facility was designed and decorated. It was not your typical sterile and corporate-looking doctor's office décor. The walls were thoughtfully appointed with artistic renderings of different dogs and cats. Several abstract sculptures and paintings gave the feel of an art gallery and created the general impression that the team of doctors who operated this facility cared as much about creating a welcoming and aesthetic environment as they did about treating their four-legged patients.

Once the obligatory paperwork and checkout forms had been taken care of, a member of the nursing staff brought Keith to a private consultation room where he waited for Jack. A few moments later, the nurse walked Jack into the room and Jack immediately pulled his ears back, happy to see Keith. He did his best to muster a few wags of his tail. He was shaved to the skin on his left hindquarters, which revealed a large incision. When the nurse walked him into the room, she was holding Jack's bottom half up with a sling. The nurse went over the procedures and Jack's medication for the next several weeks during his recovery.

"The operation was a complete success," she told Keith. "He did wonderfully and has been a great patient," she added. "He will have to be sling-walked for several weeks, until he begins to gain some strength and stability in his right hip," she explained. "Jack is not in any pain from the grinding hip any more. He will feel some soreness and tenderness, but we have some pain medication that you can give him along with his antibiotic."

"What is sling-walking?" inquired Keith, unfamiliar with that term.

"The way I was helping him with this sling under his belly. It helps to give him support until he is able to put his full weight on the joint and until the muscles and tendons become stronger," she explained. "Basically it's just a beach towel, wrapped under his belly when you walk him out the back door and down into the back yard. You'll need to do this until he can gradually put more and more weight on his rear hips. He will probably always have a little bit of instability in that joint, but other than that, once he's recovered, he will gain more mobility through exercise, and his joint will become stronger from the strengthened muscles and tendons," she finished.

The nurse wrapped up her explanation of what to expect with Jack and how he should progress. Finally, it was time for Keith to try the sling walk himself and walk Jack out to the waiting minivan. Keith had taken the van so that Jack would not have a high step, up into the vehicle. He had removed both of the two rear seats, so that the entire back of the van was an open flat area where Jack could lay.

"Come on big guy," Keith encouraged Jack. "Let's go home." Unfortunately, the floor in the entrance area of the hospital was made of slippery tile that Jack did not seem to like. The nurse grabbed a strip of carpet that was a long runner and brought it toward the entrance of the consultation room. Keith walked Jack up to the edge and Jack began to move forward cautiously on the carpet. Jack moved along that twenty-foot stretch of carpet, which ended at another long stretch of carpet, which ran the length of the main check-in counter. After moving to a third section of carpet, which led directly to the front door, Keith was finally able to help Jack onto the concrete sidewalk outside, where Jack felt more comfortable that his weak hip would not slide out from underneath him. The nurse followed the pair out to the minivan, to ensure that Keith was successfully able to lift Jack up into the van without incident. Once Jack was securely in the van, Keith waived goodbye to the nurse and drove off from the hospital.

Jack's recovery began on Thanksgiving Day. Since it was about a ninety-minute ride from the hospital, Linda called Keith on the cell phone to find out how he was progressing. When Keith finally pulled into the Barnes driveway, all three children and Linda were waiting out front to see their beloved Collie patient.

"Happy Thanksgiving guys," proclaimed Keith as he stepped out of the van.

"Happy Thanksgiving Daddy!" returned Sandra with a wide grin wiping across her face.

"I have a big, furry Thanksgiving gift for you guys. He's anxious to get out and see you," announced Keith. "Remember we can't pet him on the rear hips because he's really sore back there. Only pet him on the head or the neck," he clarified.

All three Barnes children ran to the van, as Keith carefully lifted Jack and carried him into the house. He walked through the front hallway and out the back door. He went down the three steps of the deck, onto the basketball court and carefully put Jack down in the grass, so that he could sling-walk him through the yard, to allow Jack to take care of any necessary business. After accompanying Jack around the yard for a while, Keith guided him over to the steps of the deck and carefully lifted Jack's hindquarters, so that he could limp his way up the steps. Awkwardly, Keith walked Jack over to the back door and inside the house. He helped him over to his large padded footstool and let him lie down and rest.

"Oh, Jack," said Allie. "You poor baby, it'll be ok," she continued. Allie put her nose up to Jack's and rubbed noses with him as she stroked his neck and back.

"I don't like the look of those stitches on his hip mom," commented Allie.

"I know sweetie, but the doctors did a great job on him, and he's going to heal just fine," said Linda.

Keith realized that moving up and down the steps was not going to be a very effective way for Jack to get on and off the deck. "I think I need to build a ramp for Jack and attach it to the deck stairs," he suggested to Linda.

Keith headed out to the hardware store and purchased some lumber and screws. He came back and got to work. Within a few hours, he had constructed and attached an eight-foot long ramp to the stairs of the deck. It went out at a gradual slope. After completing the ramp, he stapled some rubber mats to the surface to give it some texture, so that Jack would feel more confident that he would not slip when walking down the ramp.

Walking back into the family room, Keith attached Jack's leash and carefully picked him up off the footstool. Jack limped forward, one, awkward, painful step at a time.

"Shouldn't you just carry him down to the back yard babe?" questioned Linda.

"No. The nurse said he needs to work it out and start getting used to putting weight on it. He also needs to move around several times per day to keep the leg from getting too stiff and to increase his mobility," Keith explained.

Keith and Jack walked very slowly out onto the deck. Jack stopped at the top of the ramp and looked at it with concern. Jack didn't move. Keith knew this would be awkward, guiding Jack down the ramp, but ultimately, this would be his means of getting up and down for the next few weeks. Keith had made the ramp about half the width of the steps, so that he could walk down the steps beside Jack and encourage him. Jack, on the other hand, was not that encouraged about the idea of moving down this long contraption, which looked completely foreign to him, and about which, he felt quite suspicious.

"Come on Jack. Good boy," Keith said as Jack just stood and stared at the expanse of ramp before him. Keith stepped down the three steps, and Jack continued to stand, looking very concerned. There is a way that a Collie expresses concern as a facial expression that cannot be fully described, other than to say that he wrinkles his eyebrows in a manner not that different from people.

The basic emotions and responses that we share with our mammal brethren always surprised both Keith and Linda. Seeing our own human characteristics and behavior reflected in creatures that we think of as so vastly different from ourselves always brought home to Keith and Linda how remarkably similar various mammal species are to us. Linda always marveled at watching female primates caring for their young and showing their maternal instincts, which are eerily similar to those of humans. She commented to Keith that, while we may think of the human race as being so much more intelligent and sentient than primates or lower mammals, at some primeval level, our social habits and customs are very similar.

So, as Jack stood, frozen and frightened of both the strangeness of the ramp and the challenge that he knew awaited, Keith continued to try to coax Jack slowly down the ramp. Keith had to physically scoot Jack forward and place his front paws on the ramp, in an attempt to help him start on his way. After some prodding and jockeying for position between the stairs and the deck, Keith took up a position behind Jack, and immediately Jack felt that his route for retreat had been cut off. Feeling the forcefulness of Keith's presence, Jack made a desperate dash down the ramp, and Keith, startled by Jack's sudden and rapid movement, scrambled to move from the top of the steps, down beside Jack as he descended the ramp to the basketball court.

Feeling stressed and fearful, both Keith and Jack paused for a moment at the base of the ramp. After recovering from the stress of descending the ramp, Jack began to attempt some form of forward movement, while Keith supported his bottom half. After achieving success in the backyard, it was time to attempt the summit, the top of the deck. Keith guided Jack unsuspectingly toward the base of the ramp. Again, Jack just stared at the ramp, both uncertain as to its purpose and somewhat fearful about being so close to such a large and unusual monstrosity. Keith nudged Jack forward, until his front paws were positioned on the bottom edge of the ramp. Not surprisingly, Jack attempted to back away or turn to the sides of the ramp. Keith nudged him forward again, and Jack kept trying, fearfully, to back away or turn to one side. Keith lifted Jack's bottom half, holding the sling in his left hand while lifting Jack's upper half with his other arm. This gave Jack complete support and convinced him that the only place he was going was up the ramp.

A few small limping steps at a time, Jack made his way to the summit of this strange wooden mountain. Jack limped rapidly from the top of the ramp, across the deck to the back door, in an attempt to move away from the ramp as quickly as possible. The ordeal was complete. Jack had made it.

Jack's recovery continued in this manner for several weeks. Every day, his legs gained more strength and became more stable. Keith and Linda took turns lying Jack on his side each day to move his right, rear leg through some range of motion exercises that the doctor had prescribed. Often Allie or Sandra would kneel down at Jack's head, caress him and talk to him calmly, while Keith or Linda administered the therapy. For the first few weeks, Jack was quite apprehensive about the therapy, but as his mobility increased, it became easier for him, and he gradually grew accustomed to the twice-daily routine.

Jack was receiving in-home physical therapy to improve his hip mobility. Keith and Linda practiced walking him back and forth and around the back yard each day. They began with a five-minute walk, for a few days, then ten minutes, then eventually took him out on the sidewalk through the neighborhood for twenty minutes at a time. Often, one or more of the children accompanied Jack; encouraged and pet him as he walked. Jack still had some limping at this point, but he no longer required the sling to walk. He just walked slowly; concentrating on each step, as he gradually worked his way up and down the sidewalk.

Neighbors on the street watched as Jack labored by, observing the effort he was exerting simply to walk at a normal pace. They followed his progress each week and felt pity for the poor Collie for having to endure such a challenging ordeal, but every day they could see Keith or Linda helping Jack work through the challenge like a real champion, determined to achieve his goal, one-step at a time.

Slowly, Jack improved. His strength, stamina and mobility increased by miniscule amounts daily. During the span of a number of weeks, these miniscule amounts added up. Soon, Jack was allowed to run around in the backyard without being walked on the leash. He ran up and down the hill almost as if the handicap had never existed. Although Jack had improved dramatically, he had developed a common, but strange looking gait. When he ran, both of his rear legs moved in unison. They worked together as though they were joined by some invisible binding. When he walked though, his rear legs separated and worked independently. Jack was far from fully confident about his abilities however, for example, whenever he wanted to climb up onto his favorite footstool to flake out, Keith, Linda, or one of the children would have to help him up and slide him toward the center, so that he was comfortably positioned.

"Dear heavenly Father, thank your for our food, and thank you for making Jack better, and thank you for letting us take good care of him and love him, and thank you for bringing Daddy home safe from work, and thank you for letting us all eat dinner together tonight, and I hope we all sleep good tonight, and I hope Nanny and Grandpa are safe, and I hope we have a great day tomorrow. Amen," offered Sandra.

"Thank you Sandy," said Linda. Keith and Linda were always so touched by how insightful little Sandra was, and how she could pull together such a thoughtful blessing and have such a sense of thankfulness. This was one tiny victory to Linda and Keith in their challenge to raise their children not to succumb to the mantra of instant gratification and endless desire for more and more, with an absence of any sense of gratitude or appreciation for their good fortune.

Thanksgiving was good. The Barnes children had experienced a beautiful lesson as Jack was spared a terrible fate, due to the family's willingness to spare him. This year's Thanksgiving provided an experience that would stay with the Barnes family and cement their sense of giving, caring and gratitude. A wonderful seed had been planted, and as the children grew, reminders of that Thanksgiving and Jack's ordeal would provide a root that would take hold in their hearts and be carried with them.

Kevin L. Brett

Chapter 6
A Good Turn

Keith had been a Scout when he was a boy. He had completely taken to heart the Scout motto: Be Prepared. It was so simple and elegant, and completely logical. Be prepared applied to everything in life. Keith saw the

155

imperative of this mantra with his work; with emergency preparedness at home for his family, or with a roadside emergency; with preparedness for self-defense situations through his and Linda's martial arts training and with countless other life situations.

Being prepared began with educating yourself as to what you might encounter in a given situation, such as a tornado or flood and then determining how to plan and prepare in advance. So many Americans, Keith thought, encountered the unexpected because they simply did not take the time to consider how to plan and prepare for a few potential situations that could likely occur in their daily life.

Since Keith had become a husband and father, he could not stand the thought that he might experience some emergency and lack the necessary knowledge, skill or supplies to manage or mitigate it. Keith believed strongly that there were two types of people: survivors and victims. It saddened him to think that so many people in America believed that the government would take care of them no matter what happened, and that the government would have the situation so well in-hand that they would alleviate any danger, discomfort or distress. Personal responsibility and initiative was part of the spirit that had built this country, and too many modern Americans were abandoning this role.

What a difference between the mindset of modern, urban America and the days of the wagon trains, where hearty, self-reliant souls blazed trails and settled the west. Keith believed that with all of our modern conveniences and our reliance on so many modern institutions and so much urban infrastructure, that we had all become too vulnerable to the slightest disturbance to our daily routine and lifestyle. Evidence of our modern dependence and vulnerability could be seen every time some major disaster occurred. Millions of people would be cast into a state of panic, catastrophe and extreme dependence upon government assistance and intervention, simply due to the lack of a small personal investment in basic knowledge, skill and supplies.

Keith thought, if more people took it upon themselves to be well prepared, there would be fewer

157

people relying upon the government in such situations, so that first responders could focus on those who really were not able to take care of themselves.

While Linda was truly focused on the emotional and spiritual well-being of the Barnes family, Keith saw a key element of his role as head of the family, to make sure that the Barnes were prepared for a variety of situations and that he helped instill that intrepid spirit of self-reliance in his children. When Wes was in first grade, Keith signed Wes up in Cub Scouts and became the Cubmaster for Wes's Pack, chartered by their church, Ebenezer United Methodist, in Stafford. Even at this young age, he taught his Scouts and strongly emphasized and practiced the importance of such basic life skills as first aid, emergency preparedness, pioneering skills, life saving and wilderness survival. Keith had actually started introducing camping to Wes at the tender age of three and he loved it. After his first backyard campout at age three and a half, cooking beans and hot dogs over an open fire, Wes was hooked. He loved the outdoors; especially the woods and he loved camping in tents. Allie and Sandra followed suit later when they were old enough and developed the same love of the outdoors. In fact, Keith had created a Scouting event for the Pack, called Survivor, after the popular television show. The event was fun-filled, challenging and exciting. Both Allie and Sandra participated as well since Keith opened it up to the siblings of the Cub Scouts.

As Cubmaster, Keith had wanted to make his Pack different from so many he had heard about. He was completely unimpressed with some Packs that offered programs that continually played to the lowest common denominator. One of Keith's martial arts masters had a saying that, "If you expect more out of a student, you will get it." Keith had conversations with parents whose boys had experiences prior to joining his Pack where they did very little and where the Packs offered a disappointing program.

For Wes and his buddies, Keith had planned and developed the Scouting program to really prepare and excite them for the opportunities and challenges ahead in Boy Scouts. He kept to traditional activities such as

camping, hiking and outdoor skills while mixing in a
healthy blend of just plain fun. Keith wove a Scouting
fabric that brought in threads of citizenship and service.
He helped his boys develop a sense of wonder,
excitement and curiosity about exploring truly exciting
avenues and topics. He had always told Wes that
Scouting was the most fun a boy could have.

By age ten, Wes had completed his time as a Cub
Scout. He crossed over to Boy Scouts in an elaborate
Native American ceremony. Now Keith was the
Committee Chair for the Troop and Wes was working on
his various rank achievements and merit badges. Linda
also became involved with Girl Scouts and started Sandra
and Allie on the path toward good citizenship, service
and preparedness for life.

Wes and Keith were at Camp T. Brady Saunders,
completing a week of summer camp. It had been an

exciting week exploring a new camp, engaging in challenging activities and improving skills begun as a Cub Scout and learning new ones. Wes had signed up for a full schedule of merit badges, including Swimming, First Aid, Wilderness Survival, Environmental Science and Archery. After his transition from Cub Scouts, Wes was rapidly gaining an appreciation of what it really meant to listen, learn, practice and demonstrate specific skills with proficiency, to be worthy of earning the coveted merit badge.

Wes, Keith and the Scouts had an outstanding week at camp and returned home to Stafford to prepare for a truly exciting upcoming adventure. They were going to be working on several additional merit badges that summer, including Hiking, Camping, Cooking and Backpacking, and many of the requirements for these badges would be earned and completed on the trail; the Appalachian Trail. Wes, Keith and the boys had to finish planning and preparation for a week-long hike on the longest trail on the East Coast.

Troop 907 was, if nothing else, a very fun group of boys. Whenever they attended summer camp or district events where many other troops were present, Troop 907 was always the last to show up for flag ceremonies. In fact, the boys in the troop had pretty much decided that walking single file, or even double file, was completely overrated. If you saw a cluster of boys straggling along a trail, half in uniform, unkempt looking and toting a blasé attitude that could be detected from a mile away, you could be certain it was 907 on the move; and it was all good. The boys in 907 were proud of their laid back, relaxed way of doing things. They focused on having fun and were not worried in least about formality.

Wes and five of his buddies had been together all through Cub Scouts. They were in the same Den and were now together in the same Troop. They were a junior-sized band of brothers. Each had different skills and areas of interest on which the others knew they could count. They attended the same school and played some of the same sports. Now they were about to embark upon a challenge that would test the limits of their endurance, strength, skill and emotions, and at the center of this adventure would be a lovable, enthusiastic Collie.

The Troop was reviewing their final checklists. The Patrol leaders had ensured that each Scout had all the proper supplies packed; ample food, emergency supplies, shelter materials, ropes, tools and so forth. The boys had been preparing for the trip for months, focusing on a variety of crucial skills, including orienteering, wilderness survival, first aid, cooking and physical conditioning.

The night before the trip, Keith and Wes were sitting on the deck at home relaxing. "You know Wes; it really makes me feel good as a Dad to know that we can involve you in these kinds of activities. I know you always have fun and enjoy them, but I always want you to remember and think about the fact that these experiences we have and the challenges and activities, are all designed to help you develop your character," Keith said. "Life is about improving your character and giving back and serving others," he continued.

"I know," returned Wes.

"You know I've told you before that there are plenty of kids whose parents either can't or won't take the time or money to get them involved in everything like we do. That's why we hope you guys appreciate what you have," he continued. "You remember when we were at summer camp a couple of weeks ago and we met that gentleman who was eighty-two years old who had been a Scoutmaster for fifty-one years?" asked Keith.

"Oh yeah, Mr. Roy. The guy who played bugle at all the flag ceremonies," remembered Wes.

"Yes that's him," confirmed Keith.

"He was a really nice man," said Wes.

"You're right. He sure loved Scouting. In fact, what you don't know is that he had a very special Troop. The boys in his Troop could not afford to go to camp," began Keith. "They were all from poor, inner-city families where, in many cases, both parents were in prison, because of drug use and other crimes," Keith explained. "Those boys were from really messed up families. Scoutmaster Roy said that those boys had never been anywhere. BSA actually provided the money for them to sign up, bought their uniforms and gave that Troop some money for equipment. It's part of something called an outreach program," Keith said.

"That's really good that they were given what they need so they could join Scouts," observed Wes.

"Yeah, you're right Wes," said Keith. "And Mr. Roy and the other leaders in that Troop were trying to help those boys have opportunities to do things that they would never have a chance to do. He works very hard to help them learn how important it is to live a good life, instead of doing the bad things that their parents were doing," finished Keith.

"So those boys have a lot to be thankful for," added Wes.

"They sure do, and Mr. Roy is really giving a lot of service and leadership to them, and that is a way of serving others like we're always talking about," Keith said. "When you become an older Scout, you can help teach the younger ones and give back some of what you have learned, so that they can have as much fun as you have."

"Yeah that would be really cool," thought Wes aloud.

It was the morning of the big trip. The Troop was meeting up at the local Dunkin Donuts on the main drag, Route 610, in Stafford. After checking the role, collecting all the necessary paperwork, and reviewing last minute details, the Troop was ready to leave for the A-T. Their destination was an entry point in the National Park, known as Thornton Gap. It would take approximately three hours to reach the location, where they would leave their vehicles and begin their journey on foot. The entire week would be a roughly fifty-mile journey south along the A-T. Once the Troop reached their destination, their vehicles would be waiting for them. Other members of the Troop committee would ferry the vehicles to the southern destination and park them in a pre-determined parking lot for the Troop to retrieve when they reached the end of their hike.

On this particular expedition, as on several previous campouts, Jack would accompany the Troop. The boys always enjoyed whenever Jack was around, and it was obvious that Jack enjoyed all the companionship and attention from the boys. It was easy to see by watching Jack walking along the trail, that he enjoyed the sights, sounds and smells of the forest. Certainly, there was more excitement for a Collie's olfactory senses in the wild than could be had merely prancing around the neighborhood.

Jack enjoyed pacing himself just a little bit ahead of the Troop. His usual routine was to sniff out the area ahead just to get a sense of what to expect. Amusingly, whenever Jack accompanied the Troop, he worked in a circular pattern. He spent some of his time at the point, then drifted back along the side of the Troop and then eventually moved toward the back of the Troop. Eventually, he began walking along the opposite side of the Troop, completing the circuit. Unknown to the boys,

Jack was herding the Scouts along. The boys and the Scoutmaster might not have been completely aware, simply thinking that Jack was just spending a little time accompanying each of them, but in fact, in Jack's mind, this was his flock and he was watching out to make sure they were all present or accounted for and safe.

The Troop arrived at Thornton Gap just a little after noon. Jack had been riding in the back of the SUV, occasionally standing up and looking between the headrests of the two rear seats. The gear for Wes, Keith and one other Scout was strapped to the roof rack, which gave Jack plenty of room in the back of the vehicle. The Troop drove through the main entrance and paid their fees. After that, they headed over to the Ranger Station for orientation.

The Park Rangers gave the entire Troop a thorough orientation to the Appalachian Trial and reviewed safety procedures, park regulations, wildlife, terrain, weather characteristics and current trail conditions. During the orientation, Jack sat on the front porch of the Ranger cabin, keeping watch over the parking lot and the general premises. Since they were in a public place, Keith had taken Jack and wrapped his leash around one of the frame pieces of the railing on the front porch and told him to stay, but the leash was only necessary, not for Jack, but for the Rangers and other visitors to feel comfortable.

A few visitors came and went during the forty-five minute orientation, and Jack greeted them with his "smile", pulling his ears back against his head and letting his jaw slightly open. It was uncanny how this facial expression resembled a smile. There was no other term to describe it, probably because that is exactly what it was. Jack alternated between this "smile" and a very alert, attentive look, with ears perked up, mouth closed, shoulders erect.

The Troop finished their session with the Rangers and came back out of the building. Jack sat patiently waiting for Keith and Wes. Many of the boys that filed by gave Jack a pat on the head, at which point; he instantly flattened his ears and just slightly tucked his head down, almost like a turtle about to retract his head back into his shell. The Troop assembled back in the parking lot and began removing their backpacks from the cars and trucks. Jack remained on the front porch waiting for them to finish. He let out a couple of barks, just as a bit of a reminder for the boys not to forget that he was standing watch and waiting for them to retrieve him.

Once everyone was suited up and ready to head out, Keith went to retrieve Jack. The Troop headed over to an entry point for the trail and entered the woods and thick underbrush. Jack was at the rear with Keith, while Wes was closer to the front of the line. As is procedure, the boys and leaders were all walking single file. This method was both the most courteous, in the event that one might encounter other hikers coming from the opposite direction and the safest, lest a hiker bump into someone beside them and send them tumbling off a narrow trail down some ravine or hillside.

On one occasion, Keith had taken his Cub Scouts on a three-mile hike along the Passamaquoddy Trail, which was farther north along the A-T. He had tried to explain the necessity of walking single file so that no one would be bumped and fall off a steep trail. The Scouts were not very quick to adopt this procedure, preferring instead to walk three or four abreast, playing, talking and having a grand time. Curiously, as soon as the hiking trail became no wider than a few inches, with a very steep drop off several hundred feet down, the boys magically began to internalize the concept of walking single file. What a brilliant idea, to avoid walking beside each other on such a narrow trail. Why hadn't one of the leaders thought of that?

Once on the trail, Keith had let Jack off the leash so he could roam or herd, and as before, Jack walked along the rear of the Troop for a while. He eventually quickened his pace, spending a few moments beside each Scout, at least long enough to receive a pat on the head and a "Hey Jack, how's it going buddy," from his pals. As they were hiking, the boys munched on trail mix or beef jerky and sipped from tubes connected to the hydration packs they carried in their backpacks. If Jack could fully understand English, he would have been able to understand three of the boys he had just passed, who were engaged in a serious discussion.

"Shawn you moron, everyone knows that Yoda has special Jedi powers that even Darth Vader is afraid of," said Jimmy emphatically. "I can't believe I have to explain this stuff to you! You're so clueless."

"Yeah, but I bet you didn't know that Batman actually used to date Cat Woman before he met Bat Girl. Loser!" defended Shawn.

"Who cares? That show was like, during the sixties. Everyone from that generation is like dead or close to it," retorted Brad.

"Hey that's when superheroes really got going dwebe. Don't knock it."

Jim, one of the Assistant Scoutmasters, overheard the lively discussion. "Ok, guys, lighten up. Let's give peace a chance here, ok?" he said, with a self-inflicted grin and chuckle that was contagious to the other leaders. The intellectual banter continued as Jack moved around checking on the rest of his pals.

Jack passed by one of the boys, who offered him some small treat, to which Jack responded with much appreciation, before moving further forward. As in the past, Jack instinctively marched his way toward the front of the line, continuing to advance until he was a good ten or sometimes twenty paces beyond the head of the line.

He wagged his tail in appreciation of any attention he received and trimmed his ears back, but he always perked them right up to stay tuned to any sounds that might be important. When Jack reached a position in the front of the line, he all but forgot about the Troop, because now he was listening, sniffing and watching.

Today, Jack was in his same routine again. He had
started at the tail and worked his way around to everyone
in the hiking party. The weather was phenomenal, with
just barely a suggestion of a breeze. The temperature
struggled to reach seventy-four degrees with virtually no
humidity. It was the kind of weather that simply
embraced you and was quite intoxicating. Only a
smattering of clouds drifted aimlessly above, leaving the
sky otherwise virtually clear. Visibility, when you could
acquire a view between the trees, was more than fifteen
miles and pristine. There was virtually no haze to obscure
the vista. The warm rays of sunlight streamed delicately
through the forest canopy, each seeking a path to the
floor. The sun emitted a dappled pattern on the parched,
dusty trail as countless strands of illumination interwove
themselves with the shadows from the overhanging
leaves. The spectacle of lights strewn across the trail
caused everything they touched to glow brilliantly and
fleetingly, before their luminance would be doused
suddenly by the intermittent movement of the ocean of
leaves dangling high above the trail.

As Jack walked alongside his pals, his white paws and ruff caught the intermittent sunlight and achieved transitory luminescence, before dimming as the scattered sunlight streaked across his white fur in the same manner as on the trail. Even the black coat that enveloped the majority of Jack's form glistened under the bright sunlight as the intermittent rays danced across his fur.

The Troop had done well for the first day. They had not started out on the trail until about two o'clock. They hiked until about four-thirty, before stopping for the day, but they had covered nearly five miles. Not bad, considering that the typical backpack which each boy carried weighed between twenty and thirty pounds. The trail conditions were good, and the terrain on this stretch of the trail was mostly flat, wide and dry.

Jack made the rounds of the camp area, checking on each of the pairs of Scouts as they set up their tents. He sniffed around and checked out the boy's backpacks and tents. As he sniffed some of the backpacks, he could readily smell the food the boys had packaged for the trip. Even though all of the food was in either a re-sealable plastic bag, or a factory-sealed heating pouch, Jack could still detect the faint scents of some of the foods. He sniffed the packs, but then politely moved on, leaving the boy's gear alone.

Camp was set up. A good campfire was going, which filled the air with the welcome scent of smoke. The Troop was cooking their dinner over open fires in their designated fire rings. The early spring and summer had brought a decent amount of rain, so the area was not so dry that it would be dangerous to have campfires. Keith was watching two of the boys preparing a tasty pot of chili and some biscuits to go with it. He chuckled to himself when he remembered that, just a few weeks earlier, they loathed every minute of their cooking merit badge class and didn't understand why they would really need to know how to cook. Now that they were becoming very hungry, the idea of cooking did not seem such a bother.

Keith recalled being back at summer camp, walking past the outdoor cooking area after eating at the mess hall. The same boys had just finished cooking their own breakfast when Keith yelled out "Good morning! How was breakfast?" One of the boys replied, "It sucked! We burned the eggs and the butter caught on fire!" Now these same Scouts were busily chopping onions, mixing precooked hamburger meat and adding seasonings and other ingredients to their chili like a group of iron chefs. In fact, ironically, the Troop had recently been to a district Camporee, where the theme was Iron Chef and they took first and second place in the breakfast, lunch and dinner categories. The Troop had won several valuable new pieces of cooking gear and stoves as a result. So, Troop 907 couldn't make it to a flag ceremony on time, but they could cook!

Jack walked casually up to the campfire, staying safely away from that strange, hot, bright orange creature, but just close enough to sniff deeply and catch the gently wafting aroma of the developing chili situation. Jack stood motionless, puffing his cheeks in and out with each breath, sniffing in the aroma as deeply as possible. He was pondering how he might gain access to that strongly scented concoction in the large pot. One of the boys doing the cooking came by where Jack was standing and put a new pot of rice on the fire. "Hey Jack. How ya doin' boy? You like the smell of that chili? Maybe we'll have a little for you to try later," he said as he stroked Jack's back with his free hand. The Scout walked up to the fire to position the Dutch oven to cook the rice that would later be added to the chili.

Dinner was always better outdoors after a good day on the trail. The boys sat around the fire and enjoyed their meal while Jack ate his dog food. After the boys and leaders had finished, there were enough leftovers to scrape together and mix in with the last bit of Jack's dry food to make a delightful dinner stew for him. Jack gobbled up this welcome addition to his food. Then he walked around to the boys, wagging his tail and politely keeping his distance while continuing to enjoy the aroma drifting from the plates of food that the boys were beginning to collect for washing.

After dinner, the Troop continued their campfire with some of the boys' playing cards. A few others were just talking about basic boy-stuff and the Patrol Leaders were reviewing the maps for the next day of the hike. A couple of the boys sharing the same tent were having some personality clashes, which happened occasionally and unpredictably. Jim had a brilliant solution that he employed to re-direct and diffuse the attitudes. He simply walked slowly over to the two bickering boys with that same contagious grin, arms outstretched wide, "Come here. Do we need a hug? Is that what this is about?" stopping just in time, but just close enough to make the boys think he was serious, but avoiding complete embarrassment of the boys by actually giving them a big hug. He would walk so close and convincingly toward them that they were sure they were about to be bear hugged. By the time they realized that he was joking and that they were safe from this un-cool display of public affection, the feud was over. These were just some of the tactics that leaders made up to keep everything on an even keel when the waters became choppy. When the threat of a hug didn't work, there was always latrine duty.

Earlier at summer camp, many of the boys were sitting around the campfire one evening when Jim popped up suddenly. He headed over to one of the platform tents where the same two older boys were hanging out. Jim had noticed a flicker of light coming from the tent. The look of the flicker did not appear to come from a lantern or flashlight.

"Guys! Guys! Put that out. What in the world are you doing?" he bellowed in disbelief. Jim stretched his arms wide and cupped his hands, motioning for the boys to come out of the tent toward him. The boys had been sitting on the two cots in the tent. They had taken an old dirty sock, tied it to the end of a three-foot long stick and lit it on fire to test out their new fire-starter flints. Jim had spotted them waving the burning sock back and forth at each other in the tent. He was doing his best to contain what could easily erupt into near hysterical laughter at the absurdity of the situation and the ridiculously funny, but dangerous spectacle he had just witnessed.

"Help me out here. Ok, alright, . . . On the STUPID SCALE, from one to ten; ok, . . . where do you think this one falls?"

"I'd give it about a nine!" responded McElroy reflexively and almost with a hint of excitement at the thought that one of his antics potentially deserved some form or ranking or judging for the quality of its creativity.

"Alright. GUYS, we want you to have fun, but this is over the top."

"Actually, it was inside the tent." responded Todd with a proud smirk.

"Ok. The tent clearly says, 'No Flames in Tent'. Alright? Don't let me see those lighters out again unless you're lighting a campfire – outside the tent. GOT IT?"

"Yes sir," responded McElroy sheepishly.

They were all great kids, but the Scout leaders obviously had to draw the line on freedom when there was a safety issue involved. They just had to keep a close eye on the pranks and antics to ensure that everyone stayed safe.

Jim and the other leaders were keeping a close watch on this hiking trip, as on all trips, to keep everyone safe. In the morning, equipment would be re-packed, adjustments would be made to the gear and the way the weight was distributed, and the campsite would be cleaned completely. The Troop was well aware of their responsibility to *Leave No Trace*. That was the motto of outdoor ethics practiced by Boy Scouts and naturalists everywhere. The seven principles of *Leave No Trace* demanded that visitors to the outdoors plan ahead, respect nature and other people out enjoying it, and make every effort possible to leave no impact on the areas in which they had traveled.

The night air brought with it a coolness that hastened a very restful sleep, especially after the initial warm-up leg of the hike. Each pair of boys retired to their tents and gladly turned in to the cozy comfort of their sleeping bags. Jack took up a comfortable position lying down just outside of Keith's tent, keeping watch at its entrance. He lay there panting restfully, listening to the sounds of the forest, until he eventually drifted off to sleep. Jack maintained his vigil in front of Keith's tent until morning, waking occasionally in the night whenever he heard some particularly noteworthy sound in the distance.

The next morning, Jack was lying comfortably on his side, stretched out, when Keith unzipped the front of his tent. Jack opted not to move. Keith grinned and leaned down to stroke Jack's soft furry side. After about the third long stroke while still lying on his side, Jack lazily stretched his front and rear legs out as though he was in mid-stride. When Jack reached the limit of his stretch, he let out a loud, long groan, causing Keith to chuckle. "Jack you big bum; time to wake up big boy." Jack just continued to lie there and allow Keith to stroke his side. After a few more strokes, Keith decided to step over his canine doormat and head to the fire to make some coffee.

Some of the boys had stayed up quite late the night before and had been very rowdy in their tents, even after multiple futile warnings from the Scoutmaster to quiet down. Keith overheard Jim waking them in a strong, stern voice, speaking to the closed up tents, "Ok cupcakes. Let's get moving. Rise and shine knuckleheads," he said sarcastically to the very worn out Scouts. Jim had spent twenty-four years in the Army, managing his troops, and it was clear that he enjoyed inflicting a little bit of his military-bred sarcasm toward the boys whenever the opportunity presented itself. He was always looking after the boys, and his good-natured teasing was just his way of showing he cared.

As the camp came to life, there was a bustle of activity. Everyone was involved in some task; be it cooking, tending the fire, cleaning, eating or packing. Jack stood watch over the camp, but also focused his senses beyond the camp's perimeter. Once breakfast was made, devoured, cleaned up and the equipment packed and checked, it was time to hit the trail. The Patrol Leaders checked their areas, and the camp was returned to its original condition. It was now time for their first full day of hiking. There would be short rest breaks throughout the day, which helped to increase the distance they could cover without over-taxing anyone in one segment of the hike.

Jack promptly assumed his duty of making the rounds of the Troop as they moved down the trail. The weather was every bit as gorgeous as the day before and everyone was eager to see what today's leg of the journey would bring. The A-T had abundant and varied wildlife, and anyone spending any amount of time on its trails was sure to catch at least a glimpse of some of it. There were black bears, deer, rabbits, an occasional fox, snakes of several species, skunks, possums, squirrels, raccoons and a plethora of insects too numerable to ponder. In short, the region was so teeming with wildlife that, if one stood still, watched, and listened to the rhythm of the forest, one could almost get the sense that it was a wild life version of New York's Time Square.

The Troop had been moving at a good pace all morning, taking several short breaks to take in fluids and re-hydrate. Now they were moving again, about to hit mile six for the day. Jack was in his favorite spot, the lead. Walking proudly in front of his pals, Jack had the best view of the trail as new landscape features and terrain came into view. He also had the advantage of a Collie's incredible sense of smell. With the wind blowing gently toward the Troop, Jack was the first to pick up the scent of anything ahead. Of course, being mere humans, the boys and the leaders would not have picked up any significant scent even if they were as far ahead as Jack. Nonetheless, Jack kept his nose in tune, alternating between a few quick sniffs of the ground, to detect any creatures that might have passed recently, and pointing his nose into the air, head raised at about a forty-five degree angle to intercept any scent carried on the breeze.

With his incredibly fine-tuned sense of smell, Jack could detect all manners of scents from trees, moss, flowering plants, dried leaves and mammal or reptilian scents. While the aromas of the varieties of vegetation was very interesting and stimulating, the scent of living creatures was most notable in Jack's sensory priorities. Whenever he detected these types of scents, he immediately filtered out and discounted any mere vegetation in favor of concentrating on the magnitude and potential direction and source of the mammal or reptile scents.

Jack could tell the difference quite readily between a scent on the ground that was more faint and possibly hours or days old, versus a scent drifting through the air that had just blown off the body of some creature moving nearby. The difference was as distinct to him as was the difference between one of us tasting a fresh carbonated drink, versus one that had lost all of its fizz after sitting out all day.

It was nearly time to stop for lunch when something suddenly caught Jack's attention. It had an intense musky odor mixed with a scent of hot fur. He did not recognize the scent, but it was definitely not vegetation, and there even seemed to be a similar scent mixed in with the stronger scent, but of a less intense or pronounced variety. The lighter, less intense scent was also quite curious to Jack. He continued to walk ahead of the Troop, wholly tuned into these new sensations. The scents gradually became more concentrated, no longer merely a hint attached to the gentle breeze. He sensed that he was close to something. His ears perked up, now thinking that he was at least close enough to distinguish some movement forward of the Troop's position and distinct from the sounds of the boys' feet trudging along the dusty dirt trail.

Jack's ears were at maximum extension and just as intensely tuned and focused as his nose. The combination of hearing and smell, minus the actual visual contact with anything that might be attributed to these sensory inputs almost created an imaginary image in Jack's brain. He sensed that something or maybe even several somethings were not far ahead or just off the trail to one side or the other. He dared not bark, until he had actually made visual contact with the creature. He was too curious to ruin the exciting find with something as blatant as a bark, but he sensed that within seconds, something was about to reveal itself. The Troop was oblivious.

The Troop continued along, taking note of interesting boulder formations and rock cliffs as they went. Many of them also enjoyed the occasional glimpses through the forest canopy of the expansive vista across the valley to the right. The boys' thoughts were becoming more focused on the approaching break and lunch. Suddenly, Jack stopped. He began to bark. His bark was loud, clear and forceful, but did not carry with it any particular sense of danger. It was more of an announcement of discovery and a general warning. He stood erect, pointing his nose and body in the direction of his find. He looked at the leading members of the Troop as they approached. "What is it Jack?" said Brian, the first boy to reach him. "What do you see?" he inquired again.

Stopping beside Jack and looking in the direction Jack was focused, Brian could see several things moving in the low bushes. They were not very big, and it was somewhat difficult to obtain a visual on them. As more of the Troop gathered around, Jack continued his barking, but began to walk forward, now becoming a little more intense and frequent with his barks. Jack began to lower his head with a more serious and defensive posture as he closed in. The boys continued to follow whatever it was visually from the safety of the trail, hoping to catch a glimpse of whatever had Jack so totally focused. Slowly, the boys and Keith moved in the same direction as Jack to keep up with him. Then Jack stopped again, this time facing directly down the trail toward where they had all been hiking. He continued his moderately low stance, and the barks were now constant and had taken on a rather agitated, but still non-fearful tone. It was as if Jack was warning whatever it was that it was interfering with the plans of his pals.

A mere second or two after Jack changed his orientation to point down-trail, it became instantly apparent to everyone in the Troop what was garnering all of Jack's attention. A mother skunk and four babies began to waddle their way across the trail a mere five feet in front of Jack. The boys gathered safely, just a couple of feet behind Jack. Jack had served as an early warning system for the Troop, detecting a possible undesirable encounter of the stinky kind. Even though the skunk had not sprayed the noxious odor from its scent glands, the boys could now all begin to catch an occasional whiff of the dank, musky odor. It smelled like a combination of rotten eggs and horse manure, but less intense. The skunks had picked up and were carrying on their fur some of their own protective scent. The less intense scent that Jack had detected, along with the dominant musky scent, was obviously that of the babies. What the boys just now smelled directly in front of them, Jack had initially sensed from a distance of nearly two-hundred yards.

The mother skunk did not appear as a typical skunk; all black, with a white face and white stripe down the middle of its back. This skunk had a white face with a white band around the neck connecting to a white chest. The rest of the skunk was black; absent the telltale white stripe, but the residual scent from their fur and the general black and white markings, which incidentally matched Jack's black and white markings quite closely, made it clear to everyone that this was a skunk. Since this was a mother skunk, the boys immediately realized that it was doubly important not to scare or anger the mom, who would certainly not hesitate to spray anyone who might threaten her offspring. Jack only viewed the skunks as an inconvenience and an intrusion on his territory and his pals' path. Never having encountered a skunk, he was oblivious to the secret weapon buried within the skunks' hind end section. Typically, skunks are nocturnal when it is hot, but something had disturbed or potentially threatened this little family, and the mother had gotten her little ones on the move.

Jack continued barking even more excitedly as if to reprimand the skunks for trespassing on the Troop's route. The boys and Keith started to back up, allowing the skunks safe passage, hoping not to make the mother skunk feel the least bit threatened. A gap formed between the Troop and Jack as the boys backed up. Jack took a fateful step toward the skunks, increasing the loudness and intensity of his message. The boys and Keith could see it happen almost before the skunk reacted. It was almost like pre-cognition, as the mother skunk stopped; the babies continued walking across the trail past their momma on the far side of her. The protective mother skunk planted her rear legs, turned her back slightly, still looking somewhat behind her at Jack. She took aim and fired. Jack caught the scent immediately, causing him to sneeze and snort while simultaneously dodging away to the left, as the slight breeze actually carried the rank odor directly across the trail.

The spray Jack received was merely a glancing blow to his nostrils. Thanks to the favorable direction of the breeze, he had avoided any of this natural aerosol spray in his eyes or on his fur. His nose still itched and stung from the intensity of the musk, and he sneezed several times to try to expel the noxious scent from his nostrils. He had been lucky this time. Nonetheless, the scent still served its purpose, distracting Jack enough to allow the momma and her babies to escape across the trail and disappear into the brush.

As the encounter ended, the Troop had a good laugh watching Jack continue to snort and sneeze several times in an attempt to remove the scent. He pawed at his nose thinking that might help. There was a general sense of relief among everyone that no one had received a direct shot from the skunk. Everyone was amused watching poor Jack deal with the effects of even the miniscule dosage that he had received. The boys realized that it could have been much worse and might have lingered with everyone for days.

After recovering from the initial reaction, Jack emitted several barks in the direction in which the troop of skunks had gone. Meanwhile, the Boy Scout Troop resumed its trek down the path, leaving Jack to finish his conversation with the long gone skunks. As the Troop began to move past Jack, he finally gave up his vain attempt to convey any displeasure to the skunk family and resumed his duties accompanying the Troop.

"Come on Jack!" yelled one of the boys as the Troop moved down the trail.

Dinner had tasted especially good after their first full day on the trail. Instead of the three individual patrols each cooking their own different meals, the Troop had designated this as chicken fajita night. They had planned their first day to arrive at a predetermined camp area with existing fire rings so that they could build decent-sized fires for cooking. Each of the boys was carrying either a

large aluminum pot or skillet for cooking or some portion
of the food or fuel canisters or small backpacking stoves
for times when they would have to cook without a
campfire. They had all pitched in and helped with food
preparation, fire building and maintenance or washing
and cleanup. As the ingredients found their way into the
pots on the fire, the scent of the fajitas wafted through the
air and into Jack's nostrils. The fajita seasoning mix gave
the campsite the aroma of a Mexican restaurant, and Jack
was enjoying every whiff of these wonderful and
complex aromas. As usual, Jack received a small amount
of leftovers to supplement his dry food. He gladly
devoured every morsel.

The boys played cards, told stories and recounted
the day's events, before turning in for the evening. Once
again, Jack took up position just outside of Keith's tent.
He was content, with a full stomach. He was ready for a
well-earned rest after helping the Troop cover the eight
miles they had hiked that day. The Scoutmaster made the
rounds to ensure that everyone was ok in their tent;
checking on each pair of Scouts, calling them by name to

take roll and to ensure that there were no last minute needs or questions before calling it a night.

A little over an hour had passed since lights out, and the boys were sound asleep. Jack had been dozing, waking occasionally, but keeping his eyes closed; consciously taking in a few deeper sniffs to see if there were any notable scents coming his way. Jack caught a slight scent that was again unfamiliar to him and interesting. He sensed that it was not vegetation. He kept his head resting on his paws, but his eyes were open and panning left and right to see if there was anything within visual range. The scent was very faint, so he was not immediately concerned. All day, he had detected the scent of various creatures, such as rabbits and squirrels. None of them was intense enough to suggest that they were close by and worthy of much excitement. He could not distinguish if the faintness of this new scent was because it was far off or because the owner of the scent simply did not produce a very strong odor. He was not excited by it, but continued to monitor it casually with occasional sniffs, filtering out vegetation odors and focusing primarily on this new odor. Eventually the direction of the breeze shifted and the scent disappeared completely, but it was replaced with the distant sound of movement. Jack recognized the consistency of the sound as being different from the random mix of sounds throughout the forest. He could not smell anything with the shift in wind direction, but he could focus on his sense of hearing to track the direction of the sound. Ears perked, he listened, but did not move. Jack remained silent, straining to extract some slight soundtrack through the darkness and stretch the limits of his hearing. His subconscious was trying to obtain a better bearing on the movement.

There was no sound. The movement had ceased. Jack grew sleepy and drifted off, all of his senses seemingly shutting down for the evening. What seemed like a few moments passed, as Jack slept, then, in an instant, he was awake. The sound was closer, but still a ways off and certainly outside the range of hearing for any of the slumbering humans. Jack now lifted his head, remaining silent. He still failed to detect a scent, but his ears now told him the direction of the sound. It was coming directly toward the campsite. Jack stood up immediately, but silently. He listened, and very slowly and stealthily, moved forward in the direction of the sound. He walked past the main campfire ring and just past one of the nearby tents. His paws made virtually no sound as he crept across the soft, dusty ground. He stood motionless at the edge of the campsite. His frame and muscles were frozen in place. As he stood there, a slight current of air rippled across the fur of his rough and his back, gently brushing his hair as though some invisible hand were running its fingers through his thick coat. His sense of sight, sound and smell all competed with each other to pierce the night and return some minute sensory input.

Jack continued to track the unknown movement with his hearing, sensing that the direction the creature was moving was no longer directly toward him, but a few yards to the left, on the other side of the next tent over. Jack walked quietly in that direction when he froze and stared face to face at a raccoon. The raccoon let out a

purring-like growl, which for him was as guttural a
warning as he could muster. Each creature was surprised
by the other, and both immediately backed away one-step
as a cautionary move. There was a split second of silence
after the raccoon growled at Jack, and then Jack began
barking fiercely and loudly, emitting very percussive
barks in rapid succession. Almost everyone in the Troop
heard the raucous. Within seconds, the air was filled with
the sound of tents being rapidly unzipped and the rustling
of the vinyl tent material being pushed aside, as leaders
and Scouts began to pile out of their tents, looking
around in the direction of Jack's agitated barks to see
what was the problem. Jack continued barking with
intensity while the raccoon tried to move to one side and
then the other, still intent on moving past Jack, toward
the residual aromas of food emanating from the camp.
Jack did everything possible to keep the raccoon at bay
and dissuade him from his objective. Jack closed to
within inches of the raccoon's face, barring his white
fangs, ready to snap at the raccoon. The raccoon swiped
at Jack's nose with his left paw. If there is one particular

weakness that a Collie has, it is his sensitive nose, which is only covered by thin fur. Jack suffered a shallow two-inch long gash on the side of his muzzle. Now he was no longer trying to ward off the raccoon, he was about to avenge this assault.

Jack lunged at the raccoon, which darted to one side as Jack passed by, snapping at air occupied only a split second ago by the raccoon. Jack turned instantly in a quick half-circle to follow the retreating raccoon. The raccoon vanished into the brush. Jack followed suit, but while the thick brush was unproblematic for the raccoon to run underneath and affect a speedy getaway, the thickness of the brush made it very difficult for Jack to continue his pursuit. Within a few seconds, the raccoon had covered a hundred yards and was lost to the darkness. Jack, trying to following in a direct line where the raccoon had gone, was stopped less than twenty feet into the brush, by a thick tangle of weeds, bushes, fallen branches and trees.

As graceful and agile Collies are, they are not built for rapid movement through thick brush. Jack realized that he was at a dead end. He stayed in place and simply continued to bark in the direction of the raccoon to warn him not to even think about coming back to his campsite. Some of Jack's pals and Keith walked up to him and quieted him down so that everyone could return to camp.

"Good boy Jack," said Keith. "Come on back boy," he ordered. Jack abandoned his quest for the raccoon and followed Keith back to camp. Along the way, Jason, one of the Scouts, was patting Jack on the back as they walked toward the campsite. The rest of the Troop returned to their tents and turned in.

The campsite was pitch-black. The sky was mostly obstructed by cloud cover, and there was only a narrow crescent moon behind the clouds. There was virtually no moonlight available to weave through the overhead canopy of trees and cast on the scene. Jason had been in his tent with Nick for about thirty minutes after all the excitement had ended. He realized that he needed to relieve himself. He unzipped his sleeping bag, picked up a flashlight and headed out a few yards down a short trail a little ways into the woods. He had just broken a cardinal rule. He did not go with a buddy. He should have woken Nick and had Nick go with him. A Scout is always supposed to practice the buddy system for safety.

Jason went behind a tree to take care of his business. He put his flashlight in his pocket for a moment while he was behind the tree. When he finished, he took the light back out and shined it down toward the ground to light up the trail. He followed the trail a few yards and looked ahead, shining his light, but all he saw was trees and brush. He stood still for a moment and panned left and right with his light, straining to see into the distance. There were only trees. He turned around and scanned the scene with his light, but it only revealed more trees. He wondered where the tents had gone. He thought he had walked about the right distance, but he realized that he must have turned the wrong way down some side trail.

At night, with only a small flashlight, the trails and trees all look the same. He returned to where he had stopped at the tree and walked what he thought was about the same distance in the opposite direction. Surely, this was the path to take him back to his tent. He shined his light ahead to light up the forest in front of him, but again there were no tents. Jason felt the hot rush of adrenalin race through his blood as the realization struck him that he was lost.

He knew that he had gone the right way, but where was camp? He stopped and thought for a moment. He was determined to find his way back. He scanned the ground with his light and looked at several different branching paths. Any one of these could be the one that would lead him back to camp. He did not want to yell out and wake up the entire camp. That would be too embarrassing. He chose a path and followed it a few yards. He scanned with his light - nothing. He backed up, returned to the spot with several forks and tried another path. This one seemed familiar. He followed it a bit longer until it ended with several alternatives.

He was sure he was getting closer to camp and chose one of the offshoots of this path. Down the new trail he went for maybe a minute. Of course, he had not even walked for a full minute from his tent to the tree where he had relieved himself. Jason was in trouble now.

Kevin L. Brett

He had tried several alternate paths and nothing had led him back to camp. There was nothing nearby or in the distance that his light could touch that would indicate that he was anywhere near camp.

He was beginning to panic. He decided to speed up his search pattern, so that he could cover more ground and more quickly try out alternative paths. He partially retraced his steps and tried another tributary path. Nothing was working. Having already broken the rule of the buddy system, he had also broken the rule about what to do when you are lost; stay put until you are found. Your chances of being found are better. You won't burn up essential energy, and there is less risk of injury if you are not moving around through unfamiliar territory, especially at night. Jason continued running through the trails, brushing branches out of his way, tilting his light up and down between lighting up the surface of the trail and lighting up the area ahead to see if he could spot the campsite. As he ran along, he tripped several times on tree roots and half-buried rocks; each time regaining his balance as he raced forward.

Jason was scared, lost and racing nervously through the woods in the middle of the night alone. He thought for a moment that this situation felt like a scene from a nightmare. He continued running along now, just trying any path that appeared wider than the last, thinking it might take him back. Suddenly he tripped, but this time he did not catch himself. He fell and twisted his right ankle on a root. Adding to his troubles, he badly sprained his right knee when he hit the ground. As he impacted the ground, his light smacked down on a rock, breaking the bulb and popping the front housing off the flashlight. The housing was broken and could not be screwed back on to the body of the light. The batteries spilled out onto the dirt and the light ceased. Jason was lost, injured and in the dark. He felt the adrenalin increase his heart rate. He feared he might become another one of those camping statistics or tragic stories that he had so often heard on the evening news.

Jason was laying on the ground in the dark, his ankle causing him quite a bit of pain. It was very tender and hurt tremendously to put any weight on it.

Compounding his difficulties, his knee had started to swell up and become very painful. The pain of his injuries would not allow him to stand, even if he could take the weight on his ankle. Now he had to determine a course of action.

Jason felt himself loosing his grip. Adrenalin coursing through his veins seemed to have an eerie way of heightening his senses. He strained his ears to bring back some sound, which seemed to be some unseen terror that was approaching rapidly. He could hear a creature of some unknown species approaching in the darkness. The sound of movement grew closer and then paused briefly before moving quickly and then moving closer to Jason's position. He surrendered himself to the grim reality that he was trapped. Jason was starting to feel more like prey than a mere victim of a banged up knee or ankle. He was at the ends of his wits. He was virtually paralyzed with fear as he peered into the darkness, watching and awaiting the inevitable encounter with the creature, hoping that just maybe it might pass him by.

Suddenly that sound was upon Jason. It was no longer some distant consideration. Jason strained his eyes in the darkness to catch a glimpse of anything. He desperately wanted to know what creature was about to determine his fate. As he focused his gaze down the trail in the direction of the sound, a dark, hulking shape emerged slowly from the blackness of the night; its fur glistened slightly in what little moonlight was able to make its way through the thick forest canopy. Jack trotted happily up to Jason and barked a friendly bark to announce that he was on the scene. Jason nearly collapsed from relief at the sight of Jack. Jack walked up to Jason, breathing and puffing in his face as if to verify that it was actually him. Jason hugged Jack, tearing up as the sense of relief welled up inside him. "Good boy Jack!" said Jason. He hugged Jack again, hanging on to him for and extra moment to savor the feeling of having a companion to share the situation with him. Jason's confidence soared as he wrapped his arms around Jack, almost unwilling to let go. Jack happily licked Jason's face and rubbed his face with his wet nose.

Jason had been creating considerable noise in the brush and he had traveled some distance, but even at better than half a mile away, Jack had heard the crash, and detected Jason's scent. It was familiar since Jason had just been petting him on the way back after all the commotion with the raccoon.

While a Collie's eyesight at night is inferior to a human's, he has the advantage of his exquisite sense of hearing and his nose; his wonderful nose. Jack could smell Jason. He followed the trail that Jason had taken from his tent, to the tree where he had relieved himself.

For a Collie with Jack's incredible sense of smell, the scent was like having a glow in the dark line to follow. Jason's scent told Jack exactly where to go to find him.

Jason now tried to stand up, but immediately collapsed from the sudden pain. He simply could not put any weight on his ankle or knee. He tried to right himself on his good leg and limp along for one or two steps, but in the darkness, Jason could not maintain his orientation and lost his balance, falling again. He sat for a moment, his confidence dashed, and in pain. Jack stood beside Jason and barked once. "Jack go get Keith," said Jason. "Get Keith," he repeated. That was all Jack needed. He understood. Jack turned around instantly and dashed off into the darkness, in the direction from which he had come. He stopped, turned around and looked back at Jason. He barked two times and then disappeared. Jason sat in the middle of the trail, alone again, in the dark, trusting that Jack would find his way back and bring help.

Jack raced along the trail, covering the distance in half his original time. Several minutes later, Jack arrived back at camp. He trotted hurriedly over to Keith's tent, stood outside and began barking loudly and incessantly as he nosed the door of the tent. A second later, Keith unzipped his tent, the Scoutmaster unzipped his tent and a couple of the older boys did the same. Keith instinctively asked Jack what was wrong, as if Jack was simply going to give him a quick explanation and fill him in. Jack continued barking very insistently.

"Jack, the raccoon is gone. Now be quiet," said Keith. Jack continued to bark. "Jack. I said be quiet," repeated Keith.

"You said he only barks when he has a good reason Keith," said the Scoutmaster.

"What is it Jack?" asked Keith. Jack continued barking, but this time he turned and started walking toward Jason and Nick's tent and the direction Jason had taken. Keith noticed that Nick was in his tent alone.

"Where is Jason?" asked Keith, as the Scoutmaster came over to the tent.

"I don't know," answered a bleary-eyed and sleepy Nick.

"Jason is missing," said the Scoutmaster. "That's what Jack is trying to tell us," he surmised. "Keith, get some lights, rope and our hiking staffs, I've got the first aid kit, a blanket and some water. Let's follow Jack," said Tim. Keith and Tim left the other adults and Scouts at camp as they headed and followed Jack. They walked briskly and quietly, trusting Jack's nose, following just a couple of feet behind him. Keith and Tim each carried a strong wood hiking staff, not because they wanted to enjoy a nice evening hike, but because they both knew that if Jason were injured, they would need to use the blanket and the hiking staffs to put together a makeshift stretcher to carry Jason back to camp. If he were in shock for any reason, they would wrap him in an emergency space blanket from the first aid kit to keep him warm.

They continued down the trail, illuminating the area with their lanterns and headlamps. The minutes seemed to wear on as Keith and Tim hustled along behind Jack, trusting his guidance completely. Jack seemed to be trotting along with a very real sense of urgency to return to Jason. Keith and Tim followed Jack through numerous branches in the trail and off to several side trails. With complete confidence, the two anxious leaders followed in silence, each wondering how much further they would go. Keith thought to himself that Jason had traveled quite some distance and had really gotten himself lost. He began to worry about Jason and wondered if he were injured, or worse.

Keith and Tim were both starting to feel a rush of adrenalin. They were not panicking about being lost as Jason had, but out of fear for what they might find. Several agonizingly long moments passed as the rescue party hastened on their way, and then Jack raced forward to meet up with Jason. He stopped and turned around toward Keith and Tim and barked three times excitedly. Keith and Tim leaped forward with a final burst of speed and met up with Jack and Jason. Keith sat his lantern down and squatted beside Jason.

"Are you alright?" Tim asked. "Are you injured?"

"My ankle and my knee hurt really bad," replied Jason, tired, but relieved. "I'm sorry. Mr. Barnes," he said to Keith. "I just needed to go to the bathroom. I didn't want to wake up Nick," he continued.

"You wandered quite a long ways off Jason," said Tim. "Let's get that ankle wrapped up, and then we'll get you on a stretcher and back to camp."

"You know, we charge for late night ambulance rides Jason," grinned Keith. Jason smiled, feeling slightly more relieved know that he was heading back to safety.

Tim and Keith wrapped up Jason's ankle with a triangular bandage, making it nice and snug to prevent his ankle from moving around or swelling any more. Then they wrapped it in a layer of moderately tight elastic wrap to help reduce swelling and pain and stuffed a couple of instant ice packs inside the elastic bandage. They used the blanket and hiking staffs to fashion a stretcher in the manner that all Scouts are taught. They laid the staffs on the ground, parallel to each other and folded the blanket over the staffs in an overlapping fashion so that the weight of the person lying in the stretcher held the blanket in place as it wrapped around the staffs. They laid the stretcher out on the ground and lifted Jason on to it. Keith handed Jason his lantern to hold on to so that Keith's hands were free to lift his end of the stretcher. Jack waited patiently for the men to finish preparing Jason to travel. The Scoutmaster called back to camp on his radio to let them know they had found Jason and were returning. Jack barked once. Then the men lifted Jason and began to carry him forward.

"Let's go Jack," said Keith. "Take us back," he said. Jack barked twice as if to acknowledge. Then he began leading the trio back down the trail in the direction they had come. By the time the group returned to camp, there were lanterns lighting up the camp to make it easy to find. A few of the boys and adults were awake, waiting and watching for the search party. Jack was the first to appear out of the darkness. He casually pranced forward with a happy look, both to see the boys waiting and to be back at camp with Jason, Keith and Scoutmaster Tim. Jason was taken back to his tent. His ankle bandage was adjusted and his knee was wrapped with cold packs as well. After the commotion subsided, everyone finally got back to sleep for the night. Keith returned to the relative tranquility of his tent, and Jack returned to his position just outside. It had been an eventful night, and even Jack was relieved to attempt to seek some rest.

That night Jack had distinguished himself, and both Jason and the Troop were grateful for his companionship and alertness. When the Troop had completed their expedition along the Appalachian Trial and returned back home, they had a quarterly Court of Honor to award various ranks and merit badges that the boys had earned during the trip. The Troop committee had also decided that one other member of the Troop deserved special recognition. At the Troop meeting that evening, Jack had been requested to be present. Keith brought Jack into the meeting room and had him sit quietly to the side. After all of the awards had been handed out, Keith was called up by the Scoutmaster. Tim also called Jack forward. Jack rose quietly and took several steps toward Keith and Tim. Standing in front of the Troop with Jack, "Sit Jack," Tim said. Jack sat obediently. "Troop 907 of Stafford, Virginia is proud to award Captain Jack-Barnes the Medal of Heroism for finding and rescuing Jason Owen and for maintaining the highest traditions and values of Scouting by displaying bravery and loyalty to his Troop." Then Tim leaned toward Jack and put the medal around his neck. "Thank you Jack," said Tim. Tim shook Jack's left paw. Jack emitted two happy sounding barks in response to Tim's comment. Everyone knew that was Collie-speak for "You're welcome." The entire Troop applauded, whistled and cheered noisily. Jack sat panting casually, wearing his medal as he observed the celebratory raucous. Then he let out two more barks.

Chapter 7
Snakes and Bulls and Limos! Oh No!

Jack had developed the habit of sleeping at the base of the stairs, on the oak wood floor near the front door. It caused Keith to recall how, when he was in school, Lad sometimes slept in the hallway upstairs at his parent's house, or often at the foot of the bed in Keith or his sister's room. In the mornings, after his parents were out of bed, Lad headed down the hall to the kids bedrooms and started nudging around. He often went into Keith's room and pulled the covers off, or stuck his nose under the blankets and wiggled his head around to disrupt them, disturbing Keith's pleasant slumber in the process. On some occasions, Lad jumped up on Keith's bed, literally standing on Keith's chest and licking him on the face intensely, not quite slobbering, but certainly spreading Collie saliva everywhere. With more than one hundred pounds of determined Collie standing on his chest, Keith was quick to try to squirm out from underneath Lad's claws and the pressure of his weight pressing down on his chest.

Often, when Keith was home from school with a bad cold, and he lay in bed feeling miserable, he was not alone. He had company. Lad could sense that Keith was not feeling well and he slept at the foot of Keith's bed all day. Occasionally, when Keith's mom came in to check on him, Lad would get up and walk over to the head of the bed, stand or sit upright and watch as Keith's mom checked his temperature or brought him some food. Lad would sit quietly until Keith lay back down to sleep, then Lad would resume his post at the base or side of Keith's bed. On one occasion, this ritual continued for a week as Lad kept vigil beside Keith's bed. The loyal Collie kept close by Keith's side until he sensed that Keith was feeling better. Lad remained Keith's constant companion through a bad case of the flu each day, all day, and all night. Keith's parents had to coax Lad to get up and come down stairs just to eat his food; drink some water and go outside for relief.

These were fond memories for Keith, but unfortunately, poor Jack, with his hip condition could not go up the flight of stairs in the Barnes house. Jack had developed a near phobia about the oak floor in the front foyer of the house. He was very cautious about walking on that section of floor because when he had been brought home from the animal hospital on Thanksgiving Day, Jack had great difficulty negotiating the slippery floor as Keith worked to guide him with the towel-sling through the foyer toward the back of the house and into the carpeted family room.

Jack had immediately adopted a most emphatic distaste for that slippery monster in the foyer. It was many months before he even considered venturing near the floor, and even then, he only dared to place his two front paws on the wood floor while anchoring his rear legs to the safety of the carpet in the living room or family room. As the months passed, gradually Jack grew more daring or more confident, or both. He learned to slowly inch forward until all four legs were on the hardwood floor. But, in a split-second, he would back up so that at least his rear legs were on secure footing, as he saw it.

It was quite some time before Jack felt completely comfortable walking on the wood floor. When he had gained enough confidence, he took up his station at the foot of the stairs. Every night after the family retired upstairs to that mysterious unseen territory at the top of that oak monster in the foyer, Jack took up his watch. For now, Jack would keep watch over the family from this vantage point near the front door. At least in his loyal canine mind, he was as close to his pack as he could comfortably get. Venturing up the stairs would have to wait until Keith and Linda made the decision to install carpet strips on the stairs. These would provide Jack the much-needed traction to ascend to the summit. Dealing with that many stairs could wait until Jack had more time to strengthen his hip and legs.

Hurricane Isabelle came along the East Coast wreaking havoc with all of its category five ferocity. The satellite imagery of this monster storm showed how the eye of the hurricane tracked just offshore along the East Coast. The spiral arms of the hurricane reached out like the tentacles of an octopus, covering the entire Middle Eastern seaboard of the United States and extending all the way up to New England. Isabelle finally made landfall around the Outer Banks of North Carolina, with peak winds of 165 miles per hour. Virtually the entire Eastern United States was in emergency preparation mode and bracing for the effects of this colossal tempest. For four days, Virginia felt the effects of relentless torrential rains and gale force winds. Nothing for hundreds of miles escaped the saturating effect of this watery assault.

Billions of dollars of property damage were the outcome of Isabelle. The four days of turbulent fury, combined with the completely saturated ground, caused countless numbers of trees of all types to be uprooted and toppled. It was as if the solid ground and firm root foundations of these trees had simply been converted to a giant mud pie with nothing more than wet spaghetti noodles holding the trees in place. These soil conditions were not capable of providing the necessary support for a tree to remain upright. Add very strong winds to this recipe and the result was trees lying prone everywhere.

The Barnes had actually lost electricity for four days during the worst part of the storm. They decided to stay for a couple of days with some friends who had not lost their power and wait until some sense of normalcy returned to both the weather and the region. Sarah lived with her husband and two sons in the Hampton Roads area near Virginia Beach. Sarah and Linda had attended high school together. They had maintained contact throughout the years and got together for visits when they could. The Barnes stayed with Sarah and her family until they had verified that the power had been restored back to their home in Stafford, returning home a few days later.

Torrential rain is not something that snakes enjoy, and while the Barnes had been gone, the wildlife population of their backyard had become slightly more diversified with the addition of one new species. An adult Copperhead, approximately three feet long, had moved out of the saturated woods behind the Barnes home, into the main yard, in search of less swampy accommodations. In the spring and fall, Copperheads are more active in the daytime, switching into a nocturnal mode during the summer and winter months. One afternoon, the Barnes children had gone outside to play in the back yard, when Jack sniffed a strange new scent that he did not in the least find normal or satisfactory.

The girls had been over on the left side of the yard. While they had been playing on the swing set, the uninvited visitor had quietly made his way into the yard. It had been under the deck and had come out onto the basketball court. Jack spotted it immediately and began to bark insanely. Jack was face to face with an adult Copperhead snake, baring his fangs angrily. The snake was coiled up in the middle of the basketball court flicking its forked tongue at Jack.

Jack barked and shifted from side to side as if trying to herd the snake to move in one direction or the other. His efforts were in vain. After several attempts at herding, he gave up on the snake and immediately headed to the other side of the yard where Sandra and Allie were playing. He began barking at the girls while simultaneously circling them and nudging them forcefully with his nose. He tried to make them move in the direction of the steps of the deck. He bent his head down low and tried to scoop upward from behind, to push them along. The girls began to move, and the determined Collie tightened the radius of the zone of control he was imposing around them. He continued to bark and nudge them along. His bark was part insistence and part concern for the girl's safety.

Immediately, Linda detected from inside the kitchen that Jack's barks were quite out of the ordinary. She went out on the deck to discover the target of Jacks' barrage of desperate sounding barks. She saw Jack engaging the snake. "Girls, stay right where you are. Do NOT go over near the basketball court. Just wait for Dad," Linda ordered. "Keith! Come here quickly!" she yelled into the house. Jack continued to bark and growl fiercely at the snake. The snake began to slowly move and position itself for whatever confrontation might ensue. "Keith! Hurry!" yelled Linda again.

Keith came running downstairs and out the back door onto the deck. There was no need for any explanation. The situation before him was immediately apparent. He knew what he had to do. He jumped over the side of the deck. While Jack kept the snake busy, Keith went over to the girls. The thought that the girls could have been bitten angered Keith and left him feeling as if he should have anticipated the possibility of snakes coming down from the woods after the torrential rains from Isabelle.

"Come here girls. Let's go out the side gate over here," he directed. Keith led the girls to the gate on the other side of the house. He unlocked the padlock on the gate. "Go on out the gate and around into the front door girls," he said. He then closed the gate behind them and came back into the back yard near the deck. "I'm going into the garage to get something to chop off its head. I'll be right back. Jack will be fine," said Keith.

He went back out the same gate he had led the girls and circled around the front of the house. Inside the garage, Keith had a sword rack mounted on the wall, above a shelf where he and Linda had a collection of martial arts trophies they had won over their years of competition. Keith decided that something like a knife or even his machete would be too short to approach the snake. He did not want to risk being bitten in the process of trying to kill the snake. He felt that his nearly four foot long Samurai sword would do just fine. He reached up for the longer of the two swords on the rack, the Katana. That sword had been given to him by Linda when he had passed his black belt exam. He grabbed the sword in its scabbard and brought it around to the back yard.

Jack's barks were like a raging thunderstorm of explosions in rapid succession. He was simply going nuts over the snake, but he was smart enough not to move any closer to it. Jack paced from left to right, cutting off any chance of the snake escaping out into the yard. Jack had the snake pinned in the middle of the court and was not letting it go anywhere. The snake raised its head, keeping his eye on Jack; neither wanted to come into any closer proximity to the other. Keith came around the side of the deck where Jack was engaged. "Jack, back! Jack, come!" he commanded. Jack turned around and came back to Keith's side, but continued to bark ferociously in the direction of the snake. If there is one thing that Collies hated, it is snakes.

Keith removed the sword from its scabbard, gripping it properly with both hands. "Jack! Stay," he commanded. Then he slowly walked forward, holding the sword only about sixteen inches above the ground. He did not want to hold it overhead in a typical Samurai overhead striking stance. A strike from that altitude would require too much time for the blade to cover the distance from the overhead position to ground level to strike the snake, besides Keith's opponent was just a little bit shorter in stature than a typical Samurai. Keith knew that this strike needed to begin just inches above the snake's head in order to have a chance of striking the snake before it moved.

Keith inched toward the snake in a very smooth, stealthful manner. The snake simply stared at Keith, flicking its tongue defiantly. Jack continued barking incessantly, making Keith's ears begin to ring with the loud percussive outbursts. Keith positioned himself for his strike. As he closed the gap to the snake, the girls and Linda watched quietly from the deck. The scene was tense, and Keith was concentrating completely on the snake. Linda broke the silence. "Careful Keith," she said instinctively.

Without shifting his focus from the snake, Keith responded, "Thanks. That hadn't occurred to me," he replied with a calm, reserved sarcasm.

After probably two minutes of slowly, patiently working his way close to the snake, Keith took a calm breath, exhaled and struck with a sudden explosive downward cut from a height of about ten inches above the snake's head. He severed the head from the body with that downward stoke. Jack continued to bark as Keith relaxed and stood up. Jack came forward, now silent. Then, after sniffing and staring at the motionless snake,

Jack let out a pair of barks at the lifeless body of the Copperhead.

It was over. Linda and the girls had stood quietly on the deck, watching the drama unfold in slow motion. Keith felt relieved, but also angry that the snake was out there on the basketball court where it could have struck one of the children. He hugged Jack. "Thanks for keeping him busy Jack! Good boy!" he said. Keith went to clean up the snake and dispose of the dead reptile.

Keith then checked carefully around the rest of the yard, poking and prodding with a long stick to see if any friends or relatives of the Copperhead had taken up residence anywhere in the yard. Jack followed Keith along as he went, sniffing for any slight hint of other snakes. Fortunately no more were in the yard. Convinced that there were no more snakes in the yard after a thorough scan of the premises, Keith knelt down beside Jack and petted him.

"You did a great job big guy. Thank you for protecting the girls," Keith applauded. Jack simply sat panting calmly with ears trimmed back in typical happy

Collie fashion. Jack sensed the appreciation and came to know at that moment that part of being in this pack known as the Barnes meant that he would need to take the lead on scouting the grounds more closely whenever any of the Barnes was out in the yard.

Jack had begun his protective duties at a rather tender age, but then again, his own parents had done exactly that for Sunrise Acres Farm when they were well under one year of age. Now Jack was beginning to learn what it meant to protect his pack and warn them of anything that he might deem a possible threat to their safety.

Behind the Barnes home was a service road connecting another section of homes in the sub-division. On the other side of the service road was a neighborhood park with a large sports field. There were still some small local farms in the area. One afternoon, Keith looked out the kitchen window just in time to see a bull standing in the middle of the large field across the street. Seconds later, he saw Jack racing from his resting spot on the basketball court, to the fence at the far end of the yard. He had spotted the bull. Keith walked outside on to the deck and called Jack, but it was to no avail. Jack was incensed at the sight of the bull. This huge creature had apparently escaped from a nearby farm and wandered around through some fields and neighborhoods, finding his way to the park across from the Barnes home, where he was now grazing.

Now Jack was having a field day. This was certainly the largest creature Jack had ever seen. Jack was pacing rapidly back and forth along the fence, barking excitedly. He stood up and put his paws on the fence, then jumped down and then up again on the fence. Suddenly, Jack took a couple of rapid steps and leaped up over the fence, just clearing its top. He landed comfortably on the other side and took off running at full speed toward the bull. Keith watched in disbelief. Jack was low to the ground, legs outstretched as far as he could reach, so that each stride he took was as wide as possible to afford him the ability to arrive at the bull as rapidly as possible. Something as large as this bull had to be examined from a closer vantage point. In Jack's mind, there was a very real possibility that whatever this thing was, it would probably benefit from some direction from a certain Collie.

Keith raced back into the house and called 911 to report the incident. Then he ran out the front door and around the side of the house through the neighbor's yard next door. The yard next door did not have a fence, so Keith was able to run through the yard quickly and across the street, trailing far behind Jack.

Keith called Jack, but Jack was busy rushing around the bull. The bull was very laid back and not too concerned about this noisy intrusion into his grazing. To the bull, Jack was just a buzzing fly. Jack kicked into herding mode and began running back and forth. He began to pat down the ground in typical herding fashion, thinking that he was going to prevent the bull from going anywhere or heading any place where he didn't think he should go. Keith was amazed by the scene. Here was a huge bull in the middle of the neighborhood park, which itself was quite a bizarre scene. Now a crazed Collie was barking wildly while valiantly trying everything in his power to try to move the bull here or there or simply make sure the bull understood that he was surrounded. The bull began to respond to Jack, moving back away. As he did so, Jack tightened the circle on him and kept pushing the bull back. Just a few yards away was a chain link backstop for the baseball field. Jack was slowly and determinedly, forcing the bull back into the curve formed by the backstop. He had the bull pinned against the fence. Keith watched in amazement.

"Jack! Come!" Keith commanded in vain, as he continued to run closer to Jack while being careful not to come too close to the bull. "Jack! Come here boy!" He tried again. "Jack! Come!" Yelling now with every bit of sternness he could muster.

Jack was too excited and focused to be concerned with Keith. Moments later, the Sheriff's department and the animal control officers showed up at the park. The animal control officer approached Keith and simply stared in amazement for a moment before he spoke.

"It looks like your dog has the bull well contained," he commented to Keith.

"Yes, and he's so focused, I can't get him to retreat," said Keith.

"Well he's already done half of our job. I'll go get my tranquilizer gun and we'll have that bull out of here in no time. Maybe once the bull is down; your dog will let up some."

"That may be the only way," Keith said with a chuckle.

For a Collie of Jack's relatively young age, he had experienced numerous adventures and had proven himself to be always alert and up for the occasion.

There always seemed to be adventure or drama whenever Jack was nearby, or maybe Jack's mere presence was the singular catalyst needed to propel the drama of the moment to its final crescendo. Whatever the case, for all of Jack's drama or heroism, things certainly seemed to work out for the better with his keen sense of purpose and initiative.

There were times, however, when Jack's presence did not always lend some benefit to the moment. While Jack was nearly two years old, he was still very much a puppy at heart. He had learned and experienced much, but had much more to learn. Manners were something that Keith and Linda had been trying to teach Jack with limited success. Jack's pirate-like personality seemed to cause him to rebel in some areas where Keith expected him to be more obedient. Jack had been learning to sit and lay down in the kitchen whenever the family sat in the dining room for a meal. However, like a child, knowing what is right and wrong and actually doing what is right do not always coincide.

Jack had developed something, whether it was confidence, boldness, or simply bad manners, was not clear, but he had certainly developed something. That something was a knack for coming over to the table during dinner and lurking like a land-shark. It did not matter if the family was eating in the dining room or enjoying a nice evening having dinner on the deck. Jack enjoyed walking around the table uninvited and absconding with any enticing delights that were not well guarded. Jack's quarry included hamburgers, hot dogs, or his favorite, pepperoni pizza. If food was on a plate that was close to the edge of the table, it was gone. Jack, on several occasions, had suddenly grabbed a hot dog from one of the girls' hands as she held it in preparation for taking a bite. One evening, Keith had just finished fixing fajitas. The table in the dining room was set. The kids were beginning to come in and take their seats. Keith had placed a plate of about a dozen warmed fajita wraps near the edge of the table. He was buzzing back and forth to the kitchen to bring out the other dishes for the meal. As he returned to the dining room, he entered just in time to see Jack hop down off the edge of a chair and run off with all twelve fajita wraps dangling from his mouth. "It's as if there is a shark with legs lurking around the table," Keith commented one night. Certainly, Jack had much to learn, or maybe it wasn't Jack that had something to learn.

Jack had an affinity for hats, and like most dogs, shoes and socks. Invariably, whenever Keith came downstairs carrying a pair of hiking shoes and some thick socks, he would sit down on a chair and put his foot down to try to cover both shoes while he put on his socks. Jack, being Jack, and being determined, tried to wrestle one of the shoes away before Keith could finish putting on his socks. Keith scrambled to get the other sock and chased after Jack. "Jack. Drop it!" began the feeble attempt by Keith to bring the spirited Collie under control. Keith chased Jack through the house until he had the quite ecstatic Jack trapped in a corner. Then Jack dropped the shoe; chase ended; mission accomplished, unless there was another shoe lying around unprotected. Such were the pranks of the Barnes' lovable and mischievous pirate Collie.

For all his youthful mischief and sometimes-exasperating antics, Jack was always the watchdog. He protected his den; his home; his pack and he did it twenty-four seven. It was mid-August and the Barnes's next-door neighbor's son was returning from abroad where he was attending college. It was his twenty-first birthday, and his mother wanted to treat him to a special weekend with his friends. She was the CEO of a small, but rapidly growing technology firm in Fredericksburg. The CEO mom decided to hire a stretch limo for the day, to chauffer the boys around for lunch, dinner and evening entertainment.

The limo driver finally returned to deliver his youthful payload around 3:15 AM. Someone, however, was not so thrilled with these late night antics. As the gleaming white vehicle rolled down the street toward their house, Jack took note of the subtle sound of the tires as they gently crackled and popped over the tiny pebbles and minor imperfections in the smooth pavement of the roadway. The limo slowed as it approached and continued a short way down the street to a point where it could effect a challenging multi-point turn to reverse direction and return to the boy's home.

After turning around, the limo returned and docked along the right curb, directly in front of the Barnes' home. The driver door opened, followed shortly by the single passenger door at the opposite end of the massive car. The boys disembarked from their automotive yacht, joking and cavorting on their way into the house. The limo sat, anchored by the curb while the driver waited quietly. Jack, on the other hand, went berserk. He sprang from his resting position at the base of the stairs, growling deeply and barking with all the ferocity that he could muster as he spied the driver out the living room window. The walls of the house vibrated as the sound of dear Jack once again echoed and filled the airspace of the front foyer of the Barnes home.

After several barks, Keith finally woke from a deep sleep. He peered outside the bedroom window in the front of the house, in an attempt to deduce the cause of Jack's distress. Keith spotted the limo, gleaming under the street lamps. Jack continued to bark deliriously. Keith looked at the clock and shook his head. He walked downstairs and quietly tried to hush Jack. It was to no avail. Jack's powerful bark did not wake the kids, but the walls in the front foyer vibrated each time Jack fired out one of his Howitzer-like barks. Keith opened the front door and was about to go outside to speak with the limo driver. He was hoping to see if it might be possible for him to move the car down the street a few yards, but before he could undo the lock on the outer glass door, the driver returned to the cavernous interior of the car and pulled forward.

Apparently, the driver was almost as annoyed with the barking as Keith and had no desire to be the source of so much canine discontent. Jack's barking pierced the silence of the night with an unequivocal message that not all was right this night. Keith locked up, closed the door and refocused his attention on calming down Jack so that the rest of the neighborhood would not be awakened by this persistent guardian. Keith reassured Jack, "Good boy Jack, good boy. Thanks for keeping an eye out for everything. Now, go lay down. Jack. Lay down."

A few more dissipating barks trailed off as Jack's crescendo faded and the ferocity subsided. However, as always, once Jack's ire was raised, it was not as if you could flip a switch and convince him that he could simply stop barking because the issue was resolved. No, it could not be that simple. Jack had to convince himself that there was no reason to continue. So, Keith headed back upstairs, knowing that Jack simply had to get those last few pitiful-sounding barks out of his system before all could return to normal. At the same time, Keith felt reassured that his faithful companion had been alert and was ready to let the family know of any possible issue no matter what the hour.

Chapter 8
Mystery in the Rockies

The Barnes loved spending Christmas at their log home in the Colorado Rockies, and they completely enjoyed the snowy climate of the region. Both Keith and Linda were avid skiers, and the kids had taken after their parents by taking an early interest in snowboarding and skiing. Their SUV, complete with Jack in the back, pulled into the small, valley town of Simpson's Creek, population six thousand and one. Looking at the "Welcome to Simpson's Creek" sign as they pulled into town, made Wes wonder who actually painted or maintained those signs. How accurate were they; not quite like a web site where each page says, "Last Updated on August 3, 2008," Simpson's Creek was a former gold mining town dating back to the 1840's and the days of some early Colorado outlaws.

Keith needed to make a quick stop in town before they headed out to the cabin. He wanted to check in with a local contactor and architect he had hired. Keith was having a wing added to the cabin for office and conference room space. This extra space would allow Keith to do some of his work from the cabin and use video teleconferencing to communicate with personnel at distant locations. Keith had been working with this contractor to try to bring the budget for the project under control because the project was taking its toll on Keith's

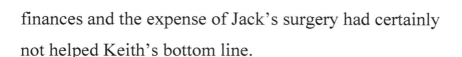

finances and the expense of Jack's surgery had certainly not helped Keith's bottom line.

Keith drove up to Hank's office and turned off the truck. "I'll just be a minute or two. Why don't you guys take Jack and stretch your legs," he said to everyone.

"Ok, Dad! Goodie!" said Sandra with a thrill. Keith headed into Hank's office for a quick status update on plans for the addition. A few minutes later, Keith emerged from the one-story brick building with a cardboard tube in his hand. Inside the tube was the latest set of blueprints Hank had drafted based on some modifications and adjustments he and Keith had discussed and reviewed.

Hank had been a local contractor and architect in Simpson's Creek and the nearby town of Mooresville for many years. Hank was in his mid-fifties, with thick, coarse, salt and pepper hair that struggled to follow a simple wave on both sides of the part in his hair. Hank was a formidable figure, standing nearly six feet-three inches tall, with a slight protruding belly that he had been nurturing for some years. He was a strong and stout individual who, in his younger years, had felled many trees with his axe as a prelude to his carpentry profession, which eventually positioned him to study architecture and become a contractor. Hank was also a combination part-time sleuth, historian and archeologist. For years, he had been researching the outlaws of the old west and studying ancient Native American sites across the state. Several of Hank's research sources had pointed toward the very real possibility that a significant stash of gold and silver was buried somewhere outside of the town, the question was where? Hank's unfulfilled fantasy was to find the gold and prove the legends true.

Back in the 1840s, when the region was first being settled, this area had been an occasional hangout of several rival gangs of Colorado outlaws. It was rumored that one of the gangs had hidden out somewhere just outside Simpson's Creek, not long before the leader was shot and killed. Rumor had it that part of his gang had robbed several stagecoaches of their cargo of silver and gold. After lightening the load of the stagecoaches, the gang had taken the loot back to a rustic cabin hideout and buried it somewhere on the premises, or so the story says.

Many theories existed about where the lost loot might be buried. Some questioned whether it had been dug up and moved somewhere off into the mountains. There was some solid evidence that Hank had uncovered from newspaper accounts of the time, that indicated that local marshals had been told that the gold was buried near an old mine shaft, but that was supposition and conjecture and the stuff of fantasies. Hank simply enjoyed digging through research sources and attempting to piece together the puzzle. To Hank, it was the intellectual challenge and the excitement of building a trail of clues that he enjoyed most. There always seemed to be just one more piece to the puzzle or one more source of information that might lead to proving this story a hoax or a real cash bonanza. Either way, the answer remained ever elusive and that continued to captivate Hank's interest.

As Keith climbed back into the SUV and started it up, the rest of the crew migrated back and piled into their seats. Linda walked back toward the vehicle from the sidewalk, just as Hank came outside and waived to everyone. Seeing Jack, Hank sauntered up to him and squatted down to pet the friendly Collie. Jack's ears folded back and he smiled in his customary way as Hank stroked his head and petted him. "Wow, this guy has really grown and turned into a real beauty," remarked Hank.

"Yes he has," replied Linda. "Although he's had some rough patches, but he's doing great now thanks to the kids helping out with his recovery and therapy," she continued.

"Well it's great seeing all of you again. Hello, kids. I'll come out to the house tomorrow and check on the progress of the addition," promised Hank.

"Great. We'll have some hot cider waiting for you," replied Linda.

The family drove away down Simpson Street, the main street in town. Everyone marveled at the beautiful small-town decorations strung across between some of the phone poles and the garland wreathes on all of the street lamps. The shops were also decorated with wreaths and garland. Linda thought the main street looked like a Courier and Ives post card, except for the lack of snow. People were walking along the sidewalks with packages and bags from the local stores, busy with their Christmas shopping. Christmas music could be heard along the rows of stores adding a merry soundtrack to the scene. As the Barnes drove toward the outskirts of town and turned on 11th Street past the fire station, small snowflakes began drifting aimlessly down from the wintry-grey sky. The flakes were widely separated; not a major event to be sure, but even so, each flake fell, silently seeking its landing zone awaiting more fluff from the sky. Now the postcard was complete.

Jack looked out the window, intently observing everything. He had been out here once last year just before his surgery. This time he would be able to play and romp in the snow, now that he was completely healed and doing wonderfully.

Kevin L. Brett

The family made their way out of town to their log home. Linda went inside to start up the furnace. "Wes, let's get a fire built in the fire place," she called.

"Ok mom," he replied.

Keith let Jack out the back of the SUV as the girls started bringing their bags into the cabin. Jack began sniffing around the property, checking out all the new smells. He scoured the ground in the area around the front door, just taking in all the scents. He did not smell anything in particular; he was just sampling different areas, looking to see if he could detect the presence of any recent four-legged visitors of any type.

The family finished settling in and Linda and the girls began making some hot chili and cornbread for dinner. Wes had a nice fire going in the living room fireplace and Keith finished looking over the current work that had been done on the addition. The new addition had a log-framed walkway that was glassed in to form a glass corridor between the main house and the addition that would be his office. Now it was evening, and as the sun began to set, the final glow of sunlight in the sky slipped quietly away into the darkness. The Barnes family gathered for a warming winter meal in the dining room.

"Wes would you go call Jack inside please?" Keith requested.

"Sure," he replied.

Jack came bounding inside the house with his smile and a slight pant. He had been enjoying himself, romping around the property. The place had been out of his Collie brain for a year, but some scents like that of the logs from the cabin were familiar, and his canine brain reconciled them with those of nearly a year ago.

"Are you thinking about doing some riding around on the ATV's tomorrow?" Linda asked Keith as they finished clearing the dinner table.

"Yes. Wes, would you like to go ride around a little tomorrow? It would give you a chance to practice handling the vehicle some more," Keith inquired.

"Awesome! Yeah, Dad. I can't wait!" said Wes.

"Ok. After breakfast we'll fire those beasts up and see where they take us," Keith finished.

Linda and Keith had been reading in the living room. It was a cozy and inviting two-story great room with a central fireplace and log walls. It was overlooked by an upstairs hallway that led to the bedrooms. They had each been quietly reading a book by the crackling fire. The kids were all enjoying themselves in the game room off to the side of the kitchen.

"I think I'll turn in," Linda said to Keith.

"Ok, be right there as soon as I shut everything down and lock up," Keith replied.

"Guys, time for bed. Let's head upstairs," Linda called toward the game room.

Everyone made their way upstairs in turn and within a few minutes, the whole family, except Jack, was upstairs getting ready for bed. Jack took up a strategic position at the base of the stairs. From here, he could look across into the great room and up the stairway while still hearing his adult masters just upstairs, as they occasionally tossed and turned in their beds. His spot was perfectly chosen. All was good. Jack maintained his post throughout the night.

The family awoke to a beautiful, sunny, winter day in the valley. Linda began cooking bacon on the open grill in the kitchen's center island. Soon everyone came downstairs, drawn by the combined scents of fresh coffee and bacon wafting their way upstairs. Jack paced around the kitchen area, sniffing at the ground just to make sure that no morsel of food had found its way to a lower altitude than the counter top or the table.

After breakfast, Keith and Wes headed out to the garage and opened it up to connect the ATV trailer to the back of the SUV. They took the ATVs further out into the valley to some open areas where there were wide passageways between the fir trees and other evergreens that dotted the landscape. They enjoyed several of hours of exploring the region. A few more light snowflakes began to fall, replacing those that had fallen yesterday.

Yesterday's snow had already nearly evaporated into the thin, warming Colorado air.

Later in the day, after lunch, Hank stopped by to meet with Keith and review the progress on the wing. Keith and Hank came into the main house and visited with Linda for a short time as she delivered the promised hot cider. The day passed uneventfully and soon it was evening again. Allie and Sandra had enjoyed playing outside with Jack just before dinner, but the sun had now nearly disappeared behind the mountain peaks, and it was time to head inside for the night. Jack, Sandra and Allie all tracked leaves and debris from the yard into the entranceway where they hung their coats in the entrance closet. At the end of the evening, Jack was once again at his post at the base of the stairs.

The few light snowflakes that had fallen that afternoon and the day they arrived had barely created a dusting on the ground. Several inches of snow had fallen earlier in December, but a few scattered clumps of white stuff were the only remaining signs of that event. The new dusting of snow looked as if it were attempting to connect the clumps of older snow to restore the previous blanket of flakey precipitation, but there was not enough to accomplish the task. Plenty of ground was still bare. Nonetheless, the two dark shapes that approached the Barnes property were not particularly concerned with trying to stay on the undusted ground to prevent the creation of any footprints in the snow.

They left their pickup truck quite a few yards from the Barnes garage. The night before, they had broken into the garage by picking the lock and had gone in with a metal detector and shovels in hand. Inside the garage were a large riding mower and the pair of ATVs on an open trailer. The two intruders had to move these bothersome items around in order to conduct a full scan of the floor with the metal detector. Two nights ago, before the Barnes arrived, they had found an area of the floor that provided a strong signal, indicating that there was some type of metal below the surface of the gravel-floored garage. That area was tonight's objective.

The garage was rustic. It was built out of different logs than those used when the main log home was constructed. The logs in the main house were carefully prepared and kiln-dried while the logs for the garage were simply cut, shaped and given an exterior treatment of preservative that had to be reapplied every several years. The log walls of the garage were built on top of a much older stone foundation that formed the outline of the current structure. This stone foundation kept the logs off the ground and provided a barrier from termites and rot. Inside, the garage simply had a gravel or chat floor.

Tonight the intruders had to work quietly so as not to alarm the Barnes family while they slept. The intruders had two battery-powered lanterns with them. They lit up their lanterns and began clearing the gravel from the "hot" spot. Then they began to dig.

Just over twelve inches below the surface, they struck a solid object. The larger of the two figures took the lead in digging while the other held the light to afford

a better look inside the hole. A few more minutes passed
and the top of a partially rotted, wooden trap door
appeared beneath the loose dirt. The digger used the edge
of his shovel to pry up one of the slats in the crude door
and then used that slat as a handle to lift the door.
Another twenty inches beneath the door lay a decaying
wooden strongbox about the size of a footlocker. The box
had iron corners and iron straps around the sides and
across the top. There was no lock on it.

The digger opened the lid to the box and quickly
scooped up many large handfuls of glistening gold and
silver coins. The money jingled and clinked, as coins slid
and banged into each other. To the two intruders, it was
music to their ears. Within a moment or two, all of the
coins had been transferred to a couple of sturdy cloth
moneybags. The second intruder backed up and knocked
over a small round barbeque gill, which tipped over and
hit the floor with a loud crash. The intruders moved
quickly to gather their things.

What they did not know was that their movements
were being monitored. A sensor system on the Barnes

property had detected the presence of the intruders when they had entered the garage and now the sensor went off, alerting the Barnes that someone unwanted was about. Jack's trusty ears were at it again. He had quietly listened to the subtle sounds and movements as the intruders executed their mission. The final straw to confirm Jack's suspicion that not all was right was the crash of the barbeque.

Jack sprang up immediately, standing where he had been dozing and listening cautiously. He turned his head toward Keith and Linda's room upstairs to direct his warning toward them. Keith and Linda both quickly vacated their bed. Keith looked out one of the bedroom windows facing the garage and saw that there was a light moving around inside the garage. Immediately, he headed downstairs with Jack.

"Call 911," he told Linda.

"You're not going out there Keith," said Linda.

"No, but Jack is," Keith replied.

Jack was already way ahead of Keith. By the time Keith was nearing the bottom of the stairs, Jack was already waiting at the door with a couple more barks. Jack just wanted to make sure Keith was fully aware of the seriousness of the situation.

Opening the door, Keith said, "Go Jack."

He waited for Jack to gain a head start before sticking his head outside cautiously. Jack bolted for the garage as the two figures ran out the garage door toward their pickup truck. Jack raced toward the two intruders, snarling, growling and barking like an angry wolf. Jack caught up to the second larger figure and bit down toward the lower part of his calf. The figure lost his balance and nearly tumbled as Jack dug his teeth into the intruder's skin and jerked his head to the side, creating a nasty gash in the intruder's calf. The intruder cried out in pain. Jack let go in preparation for a second slashing bite, but the intruder's heel caught Jack in the face. Jack snorted briefly as he smarted from the accidental back kick from the intruder. The large perpetrator sprang to his feet and dashed away while Jack was temporarily distracted by the kick to the face.

Kevin L. Brett

Jack shook his head for a second, which was all the time the intruder required to reach the pickup truck, jump inside and slam the door shut. Jack barked and ran after the truck, but the first intruder was already behind the wheel and started the getaway vehicle while the second intruder was being assaulted by Jack. With both intruders safely inside the truck, Jack continued running after the vehicle, barking as it slipped and skidded down the gravel road leading away from the Barnes's cabin.

As the driver smashed the gas pedal to the floorboard, the truck swerved and swished on the slippery and loose roadway. The truck slid off the edge of the road, and the right front corner of the truck hit the edge of a tree, smashing in the corner of the bumper and half crushing the corner of the front fender that housed the headlight. The headlight was also crushed and put out during the glancing blow the truck made against the tree trunk. The driver jerked the wheel to the left, which caused the rear end to swing to the right, almost smacking the same tree with the rear of the truck as it sped past and re-centered itself on the roadway. The

260

truck disappeared into the night, with Jack barking after it.

"Jack! Come!" commanded Keith. Jack stopped in his tracks, issued a few more angry barks and then turned around slowly. He began walking back toward the house. Keith felt frustrated that he could not catch the culprits. "Good boy Jack! Good boy!" Keith praised Jack as he pet and stroked him on the back. "You did good buddy."

About ten minutes later, a Sherriff's deputy appeared at the end of the long driveway leading to the property. Jack saw the flashing lights and started barking as if his intruders had returned. Jack and Keith were back inside the house. When Keith saw the deputy pull up toward the house, he went outside to greet him.

"Looks like we had a break-in officer," Keith offered.

"Is everyone ok?" he queried.

"All safe and secure. The culprits broke into the garage. They escaped after our Collie started barking when they made some loud noises. I think Jack got a bite into one of their ankles or lower legs," Keith explained.

"So there was more than one of them?" inquired the deputy.

"Yes. It appeared that there were two of them."

"Did they have a vehicle?"

"Yes, a pickup truck. In fact, if you find a pickup truck with a smashed-in, right-front end, you'll most likely have the culprit."

"Have you checked inside the garage to see if anything was taken?"

"No. Not yet."

"Let's check it out so that I can include that in my report," said deputy Metcalf.

Keith and the officer walked over toward the garage. Linda came out a moment later to see what was so interesting to the intruders. The party headed into the garage and flipped on the lights. They looked around for a moment before they spotted something quite unexpected.

"Keith. Over here," called Linda. A foot from where she was standing was the dugout hole that the intruders had left. The strong box was still inside, the trap door was tilted back and leaning against a small pile of dirt the intruders had dug up.

"What in the world is this?" wondered Linda.

"Looks to me like an old west type of strong-box," observed the deputy.

"What would that have been used for?" asked Linda.

"Money and valuables," posited the officer.

"So the intruders came in here and dug a hole, which led them to a trap door, which concealed the strong box," recapped Keith. "How did they know that it was here?" he wondered out loud.

"That is the mystery," observed the deputy. "So we need to figure out who they were; what they took; and how they knew it was there. I'll fill out my report, and tomorrow afternoon maybe we can meet for a while for a few more questions if that works for you folks," inquired the deputy.

"That would be fine," replied Keith.

"Looks to me like you have a pretty effective alarm system," the deputy said as he looked down at Jack sitting quietly. The deputy bid them good night and left them to lock up the garage and return to the cabin.

The next day, Linda took the SUV into town to pick up some groceries. As she passed by Hank's office, she noticed a pickup truck. Its right front headlight and fender were smashed in. When she returned to the cabin, she told Keith what she had seen. It seemed suspicious to both of them.

"I'll take a closer look when I go to meet with him this afternoon to review the blueprints. We don't know that it was definitely his truck, so we can't assume anything," Keith said.

A while later it was time for Keith to head into town to meet with Hank. He started up the SUV and drove to Hank's office. Parked in the alley was a pickup truck with Hank's company logo on the door. The headlight and fender on the right side were smashed in. Keith looked briefly at the suspiciously damaged vehicle, as he walked toward the entrance.

"Morning Hank," called Keith, as he walked in the front entrance of the small contracting shop.

"Hey Keith, come on in," Hank replied. "I've got a fresh pot of mud ready if you're interested."

"Hey, you know me. My motto is, give me coffee and no one gets hurt," Keith joked in an attempt to relieve his mounting nervousness.

"Coming right up," Hank headed to a small alcove recessed in the back wall of the office. It housed a kitchenette with a coffee maker. A moment later, the large, burly, former lumberjack came over to Keith, who had taken a seat at a large conference room table, and handed him a fresh cup of coffee.

"Thanks. I reviewed the blueprints yesterday. They look good, and the cost estimates seem reasonable."

"I think we'll be able to get the rest of this project finished without any other financial surprises. I also have some suggestions that I'd like to show you about how to route some of the power and network conduits for the conference room."

Keith tried to act very nonchalant. "I noticed that you're truck looked like it was hit by something. What happened?" acting concerned, but hoping to obtain more information about last night's break-in.

"Oh that. One of my employees took it on a job site and banged it into a tree," Hank replied.

"Wow. Hope no one was hurt," Keith offered.

"No, just the truck," Hank said. As he replied, his eyes shifted away, avoiding eye contact. Immediately this sent up more of a suspicion flag in Keith's brain. He wondered what Hank was hiding and why he would have broken into his garage. As Hank walked around the table to retrieve the blueprints from his drafting table, Keith noticed that Hank appeared to have somewhat of a limp.

"You ok Hank?" Keith asked.

"Yeah, I slipped on some of that light snow that we got yesterday and twisted my darned ankle. It was real slick stuff," he explained.

Keith wasn't completely buying it. They reviewed Hank's suggested modifications to the routings for the conduits, which required some minor changes to some of the interior molding and woodwork. Keith agreed to the changes. About thirty minutes after he had arrived, Keith was on his way out of Hank's office. He bid him good afternoon and headed back to the cabin.

"Well, I saw the smashed in headlight and I noticed something else during my meeting with Hank," Keith explained to Linda. "When he was walking around, he had a noticeable limp; said he got it when he sprained his ankle from a spill he took on some of that slight dusting of snow we got the other day."

"Hmmm," pondered Linda.

"I'm thinking his limp was caused by a certain Collie dog that got a piece of him."

"Should we call the deputy and let him know?"

"I don't know. We need to think about it a bit. We probably need to give him time to work with what we've already told him, before complicating the situation."

"Yeah, maybe so," agreed Linda.

"It's past lunch time. Why don't we gather the kids and go have lunch at the Caribou Café?"

"Sounds good to me. Kids, come on. Get your coats. We're going out for lunch."

A moment later, the three Barnes children filed into the kitchen en route to the coat closet.

"Do we really need our coats Mom?" questioned Wes. "It's not even cold outside. It's so warm and sunny."

"Just take them with you honey," said Linda. "You know how a storm front can come in very suddenly through the mountains."

"Can we take Jack? Please?" begged Allie. "Since it's warm out, we could eat outside at the outdoor tables and have Jack with us."

"I suppose that would be ok," decided Linda.

"Yeah!" squealed Allie.

Everyone piled into the SUV. Keith opened the rear hatch and Jack hopped up inside. The whole Barnes clan was now aboard and ready for departure.

The Caribou Café was a local favorite. The family had been there a number of times. The Barnes requested a table outside as Allie had suggested. The café was a rustic and cozy affair with outdoor seating near the street and around one side of the building. The restaurant was a stone and log design that was reminiscent of a mountain hunting or ski lodge. Keith attached Jack's leash to the ornate cast iron fence that enclosed the outdoor eating area. Around near the various tables were tall propane area heaters that roughly resembled lampposts. These heaters added a bit of warmth to take the chill off the air and they made the outdoor café a comfortable destination even on a cool day.

"It's hard to believe that Christmas Eve is in two days," commented Keith. "I always love being here for Christmas. The small-town feel just seems more restful than all the commotion and rush of the suburbs and the city."

"I love it here too," added Wes. "It's like the way everyone should be able to celebrate, just focusing on family and having fun together and taking a break from school and work."

"Yeah. It would be nice if everyone had time off for a couple of weeks. But then we wouldn't be able to come and eat here 'cause they'd be closed!" Keith joked.

"I can't wait to open presents!" giggled Sandra.

"What if you don't get any; nerd face," teased Wes in his typical, pestering big brother fashion, proud of his annoying quip at his little sister. "Maybe you haven't been good enough this year," he said, adding insult to injury.

"I have too been good – mostly," defended Sandra.

Linda froze; giving Wes a look that clearly told him that he had said enough. She had her chin tucked down and eyes looking intently at him to make sure that he saw her dissatisfaction. After a momentary silence, during which Linda administered her motherly look toward Wes, she said, "Let's remember the reason for the season and focus on how important it is to be thankful for the gifts we receive every day. We need to remember to share Christmas with others who are not so lucky. If we do that, then it doesn't really matter where we celebrate or what we receive. We just have to practice the important things, like being generous and helping others."

A moment later, the waiter came to the table. "Hello. I'm Byron. Welcome to the Caribou Café. Can I start you folks off with some drinks? Maybe some Caribou juice for the kids?"

"Caribou juice!" exclaimed Sandra in a startled manner. "Where does THAT come from?" she inquired with concern.

"You don't want to know, nerd butt," interjected Wes lovingly. "It's when the Caribou lifts his leg and . . ."

"Enough Wes!" interrupted Linda. "I think YOU need some sleeping juice."

Byron grinned nervously, waiting for the air to clear, so that the parents could begin ordering the food. The family placed their order for drinks and appetizers. A few minutes later, Byron returned with the drinks. Jack was lying down on the pavement on the other side of the cast iron fence that separated the eating area from the sidewalk. He made a low cautionary growl; nothing particularly noteworthy, but Keith heard him. He figured Jack saw another dog across the street or something.

A little while later, the appetizers arrived and Byron placed them on the table with some extra plates and silverware. Jack growled again, this time a little lower and longer than the first time. Byron paused for a

Jack: The Christmas Collie

split second and looked at Jack, as he finished delivering the goods. Keith ignored Jack since he was not being disruptive.

The family enjoyed a delicious lunch and some actual enjoyable family conversation. It was possible to do so. The Barnes appeared to be actually having a rare family moment. Linda always made a mental note when all three children were actually getting along and not calling each other names or bickering, as siblings so often do. These enjoyable moments made her and Keith feel, overall, as parents, they were on the right track and that things were going well domestically; even if Sandra was a nerd butt.

Byron returned toward the end of the meal. "How was everything?" he queried.

"Delicious. That pulled pork sandwich was awesome," returned Keith.

"So, are we thinking about dessert? We have some Caribou cake that's irresistible," said Byron.

"Oh no!" fretted Sandra. "Is that made of Caribou?"

"Yeah, dumb head. It comes from the …"

"Wes!" exclaimed Linda. "ENOUGH. Just stop. We've had a very nice meal. Don't ruin it. - Sorry Byron," Linda offered.

"It's quite alright," said Byron grinning at Wes. "And no, the Caribou Cake is not made from Caribou. It's actually chocolate," explained Byron.

"Yeah right," said Wes under his breath, half-giggling.

Linda just stared at Wes, then looked at Byron. "Could you maybe put him to work in the kitchen for a few days?" Linda joked to Byron. "Maybe we'll come back and pick him up after Christmas."

"Sure thing," joked Byron, sensing her sarcasm. "We could teach him how to make Caribou Cake if you'd like," he teased.

"I think we'll pass on dessert," said Keith.

Suddenly Jack jumped up from his laying position and emitted one loud bark. He looked directly at Byron and barked and then at Linda as he barked angrily again.

"Jack! Down," Keith commanded. Jack, being a Collie and usually having to have a good reason to follow some orders, did not sit immediately. He barked toward Byron two more times, angrily with a moderately fierce growl, sandwiched between the two barks. Then he reduced his output to just a low, angry growl, before he quietly lay back down.

"What was that all about?" asked Linda.

"He probably smelled my dog. I have a German Shepherd," offered Byron quickly.

"Maybe he didn't want Wes making Caribou Cake!" joked Allie, getting one in on her brother.

"We'll just take the check please," requested Keith.

"I'll have that right out for you sir," promised Byron.

The family finished up at the café and headed down the street for a little window-shopping. The Barnes stopped into several shops along the street. At each stop, Wes waited outside with Jack, who sat properly and waited patiently for the rest of his pack to return. As the family finished their leisurely shopping, they headed back toward their SUV parked near the Caribou Café. As the SUV headed down the street, Keith noticed a deputy's car parked outside of Hank's office. As they approached Hank's office, Keith saw the deputy escorting Byron, in handcuffs, outside toward the waiting Sheriff's car. Keith was surprised and drove on by so that the kids would hopefully not notice Byron being removed in handcuffs and arouse any concern on their part.

The family returned to their cabin. Shortly after they arrived, there was a phone call from the Sherriff department. It was the same deputy who had responded to their call the other night. He requested that Keith come to the local Sherriff's office. Keith promptly headed back into town. When he arrived at the Sherriff's office, he was greeted at the front counter by Deputy Burt Metcalf.

"Hello Mr. Barnes. Thanks for coming down so quickly. I thought you would want to know what was going on as soon as I knew anything," said Metcalf.

"What's this all about officer?" Keith asked.

"I believe we've found your intruder from the other night, or at least one of them."

Deputy Metcalf motioned for Keith to follow him around the corner, where they had an interrogation room with a one-way mirror. As they walked down a narrow hallway toward the back of the office, Keith could see someone through the one-way mirror. He was seated at the table, waiting alone in the room.

"We brought him in just a half hour ago; name is Byron Tolson. He's a local," said the deputy. "We picked him up over at Mike's Coin Emporium."

"I don't understand. What does that have to do with the break-in we had the other night?" asked Keith.

"Mike called us when Byron there came in with a couple of large bags of gold and silver coins that he wanted to sell. Mike was sure he could not have come across that large of a stash of treasure legally. Mike had heard about the break-in at your place and put two and two together," explained Metcalf. "Do you recognize him from the other night Mr. Barnes?"

"No, but he was our waiter at the Caribou Café a couple of hours ago. How do you know he got the coins from our place?" Keith asked.

"Simple. He confessed. Didn't hesitate a bit, just spilled the whole story; really quite a tale," said Metcalf.

"Can we speak with him? I'd like to find out what this is all about," requested Keith.

"Sure thing, let's go in," offered Metcalf. "Byron. This is Mr. Barnes. The man whose property you were on the other night when you took the treasure. You want to explain to him what this is all about?" asked the deputy.

"Like I was telling the deputy, that land your cabin is on used to belong to my great grandfather. I heard that Hank had been doing research on local hideouts in Colorado that had been used by some early bands of Colorado outlaws. I knew that the land my great grandfather owned used to have an old cabin on it. Your garage is built on the stone foundation of the old cabin. I did some checking with relatives and found out about it. There were some rumors that some loot had been buried somewhere on the property. I just didn't know where, but

I figured it might be somewhere inside the cabin, so I broke in the old garage and used a metal detector and that's when I found it."

"So, it was you who was driving the pickup truck that night," realized Keith.

"Yeah," admitted Byron. "That cabin had been in my family for generations before the land was sold. It finally burned down and all that was left was the foundation. That's when the new property owners built that old rustic garage on the foundation in its place," continued Byron.

"So, you actually solved the mystery that Hank has been tracking for years," observed Keith.

"Guess so. There was a whole strong box full of Morgan silver dollars and Double Eagle gold coins; some of the loot that the outlaws had stolen from their different heists. I just wanted to get that loot and get the cash for it. That's when I finished work at the Caribou Café and went over to Mike's coin shop to see if he'd buy the coins," said Byron.

"So you used Hank's pickup truck that night,"
asked Keith.

"Yes sir. I work for him part time," replied Byron.

"So would you like to press charges Mr. Barnes?"
inquired Deputy Simpson.

"Charges for what?" asked Keith.

"Breaking and entering, trespassing, grand theft,"
said the deputy.

"You say the property had been in your family for
generations; right Byron?" asked Keith.

"Yes sir," replied Byron confused.

"Is that correct Deputy?" asked Keith.

"Yes that is true, but —"

"Then I don't see the problem," Keith said. "As far
as I'm concerned, Byron was just finishing cleaning out
his relatives' property that had been accidentally left
behind. After all, the loot from the outlaws had been
stored there so long ago that there's no way to trace it to
wherever it had been originally stolen, so it belongs to
Byron's family the way I see it," Keith said matter-of-
factly. "I don't see how we can press charges for

someone simply going and retrieving their own property," finished Keith.

"You serious Mr. Barnes?" asked Byron, dumbfounded.

"Your ancestors used to own the property. That treasure was part of the property and you were reclaiming it. As far as I'm concerned, no crime was committed deputy. I don't know why you're detaining this young man. I believe he has some treasure business to transact with Mike over at the coin shop," winked Keith toward Byron.

"Understood," replied Deputy Metcalf, shaking his head with a grin.

"Thank you so much Mr. Barnes. I won't forget this," pausing as he got up from the table to shake hands with Keith. "Merry Christmas," said Byron awkwardly.

"Merry Christmas Byron," returned Keith.

Keith returned to his cabin. He explained the whole episode to Linda. She agreed with what Keith had done.

"Looks like Jack recognized Byron's scent when he started barking at him at the Caribou Café," observed Linda.

"I told you he never barks without a reason," finished Keith.

The next day was Christmas Eve. A storm was expected and the Barnes had plans to attend Christmas Eve services at church. The Barnes were all busy about the house, each involved in something different, when the doorbell rang. Jack jumped up from resting in the great room and trotted to the door with a couple of happy barks, as if to announce to anyone who had not heard the doorbell that there was a visitor. Linda answered the door. It was Byron. Jack barked fiercely at the sight and scent of the intruder from a few nights ago.

"Good morning Mrs. Barnes," said Byron.

"Good morning Byron. What can I do for you? Jack go!" she commanded, trying to get Jack to back off.

"Just wondered if Mr. Barnes was around. I wanted to thank him for what he done for me yesterday," said Byron.

"Sure, come on in. I'll get him," said Linda. "Sorry. Jack is still a bit apprehensive. Jack. It's ok. Good boy," she consoled the very concerned Collie.

Clearly, Jack was confused as to why she would allow someone into the house that he had just recently chased off the property, but it wasn't Jack's place to question the logic of his human masters. He simply walked back over to where he had been laying down, this time keeping a concerned eye out for any movement on the part of this visitor that might warrant Jack's attention or intervention. Keith came downstairs to see Byron waiting near the entrance.

"Hello Byron. How's it going?" called out Keith, as he came down the steps from the upper level.

"Oh just fine Mr. Barnes. Sorry to interrupt your business, bein' Christmas Eve and all," said Byron.

"Oh, not a problem," returned Keith.

"Your house looks like a postcard Mrs. Barnes," complimented Byron.

"Thank you very much Byron," Linda said.

"I just wanted to come by and thank you for what you done yesterday at the Sherriff Department. That was real kind of you to pardon me for crossin' your land and breaking into your garage," explained Byron. "I was thinking that it wasn't right and all for me to just keep that money, and I wanted to come and return it to you if you'd be agreeable to take it," he continued.

"Absolutely not," said Keith. "I told you yesterday, that money is yours. You keep it."

"Well. I just wanted to offer it since you let me go yesterday," replied Byron.

"I appreciate the gesture," said Keith, "but it's completely unnecessary. You are to keep that money. It's been in your family way too long. It's just been misplaced for a long time, that's all."

"Well. Is there something I can do for y'all? I mean. I'd like to repay the favor somehow and set things right. What can I do for you?" he tried.

"I am a little curious who the other person was who was with you that night." inquired Keith.

"Oh," he said, looking down sheepishly toward the floor to avert Keith's eyes. "It was my Mamaw," confessed Byron. "She helped me by driving the truck so's we could get away in time. Good thing too, since Jack is so fast," concluded Byron. "Is that all? Isn't there something I can do for y'all?"

"Well. Maybe there is something," thought Keith aloud.

Linda looked quizzically at Keith, wondering where he was going with this.

"Is there anything you've really wanted to do that you didn't have the money to do? I mean something you're really passionate about; something you've always dreamed of doing," inquired Keith.

"Well. I've always been real interested in Native Americans and their history. You know there were once lots of Indians around these parts, before the white man came and took over, and there are lots of Indian sites around here," said Byron.

"That sounds pretty interesting, but how would the money help you? I don't see the connection," wondered Keith.

"Well my Pampa, had told me the stories of the old west outlaws and the treasure I found on your property. He also told me about the different Indian tribes in the state. He used to tell me about archeology and Native American history. Got me real interested," explained Byron.

"Well, there definitely is plenty of history around here. So what is your plan?" asked Keith.

"I'd like to be an archaeologist and study the history and go to the digs and the sites, but I figure I'll need to work on getting a college degree if I plan to work in that field," said Byron.

"Well. I think you certainly have the money to pay for that degree now Byron. I think you should go for it," said Keith. "Whenever you have a passion for something, that's a pretty clear signal that that's what you should be doing. If you love what you're doing it'll seem easy," explained Keith.

"Thanks for encouraging me. That's what I'd like to learn and do," said Byron.

"I hope you stay in touch and let us know how your studies are going Byron. We'd love to hear about it," interjected Linda.

"And if you need any help looking for universities that might have good history and archeology programs, I'd be happy to help you find some good ones," offered Keith.

"Well. I sure appreciate your support, and again I apologize for messing up your Christmas with all this," said Byron.

"You haven't messed up anything Byron. We're glad to see that you'll be putting the money to good use and chase your dream," said Linda.

"Thanks again folks. Merry Christmas," said Byron.

Kevin L. Brett

"Merry Christmas," replied Keith and Linda in unison.

They walked Byron to the door. Jack got up and came over, wagging his tail. Byron patted Jack on the head after shaking hands with Keith and Linda.

Later that day, a low-pressure front moved in and with it a frigid breeze that was channeled directly through Thompson's Gap. Thompson's Gap provided a direct path from the northwest through the mountains. It was through this pass that a steady stream of Canadian air began to blow. Linda saw on the local news channel that the weather forecast called for temperatures to drop into the teens overnight, and a storm front was expected to move in behind the low-pressure system, bringing significant accumulations of snow.

The next morning was Christmas Eve. The Barnes family woke up to more than two feet of new fallen snow, and it was still snowing.

"Daddy is Santa Claus going to be able to get through the snow?" asked little Sandra.

"Now Sandra, you know that Santa always finds his way. Especially since he has Rudolph's nose to light the way," said Linda.

Christmas Eve afternoon, the snow finally ended.

"Hey gang. Time to get dressed and ready for Christmas Eve service," called Linda to the children.

The family finished getting ready and finally departed for town. They attended a local church when they were in town. The congregation observed an eight PM candlelight service for Christmas Eve. As the Barnes family stood in the third row pew of the chapel, Linda noticed Byron in the same row across the aisle from the Barnes. Byron was in unison with the chorus and the rest of the congregation as they sang. After the service, the Barnes met up with Byron.

"Merry Christmas Byron," said Linda.

"Same to you M'am," replied Byron. "I'd like you to meet my Mamaw, Miss Linda," he said.

"Pleasure to meet you M'am," said Linda. "Merry Christmas."

"Merry Christmas to you too Mrs. Barnes," said Byron's grandmother. "Thank you Mr. Barnes for helping Byron and encouraging him with his school. That's a great thing."

"It looks to me like you will soon have some type of historian or archaeology researcher on your hands – another Indiana Jones for sure. Maybe he'll discover another hidden treasure or unlock some long lost secrets of the past."

"I wouldn't be surprised," she smiled.

The two families parted ways and left the chapel. The Barnes got in their SUV and headed back to the cabin, where Jack was waiting inside for them.

The next morning, the family awoke and went downstairs. Packages were laid out under the Christmas tree. One package was slightly damaged and torn partly open. Jack had been busy already.

"I guess Jack found the present with Christmas dog treats," laughed Keith. "Hey. Collies have to have a Christmas too!"

"Can Jack read the label? How did he know that present was for him Daddy?" wondered Sandra.

"I think his nose did the reading for him," intervened Linda laughing. Jack barked as Keith knelt down to help him finish opening the package. Once it was opened completely, Keith handed Jack one of the treats. Jack gratefully gobbled it up.

"Merry Christmas everyone," exclaimed Linda. Jack barked happily two times with his trademark smile and ears pinned back.

"Merry Christmas to you too Jack!" said Keith. Jack barked two more times; getting in the last word - bark.

Kevin L. Brett

Epilogue: A Great Beginning

He did not always display the utmost of intelligence, as is commonly associated with the Collie breed. He barked, at times insistently, inside the house at sounds heard upstairs, as the family simply went about typical activities. In fact, EVERY, SINGLE, NIGHT, when Keith or Linda went upstairs and lowered the window blinds in their bedroom, Jack began a several minute incantation of barking as the pull cord slid upward, allowing the blinds to be lowered to the bottom of the window sill. As the blinds slid down, the small gears inside the mechanism that lowered the blinds made a whirring sound that reverberated slightly through the drywall of the bedroom, just enough to make Jack insane with curiosity about that sound. This routine was simply part of going to bed every night and suffering through Jack's chorus of barks until he finally settled down several minutes after hearing the blinds go down. The routine never varied. At least Jack was consistent.

Jack had a large dog bed, shaped like a huge pillow. He often whined, whimpered and even barked when he was ready for the family to head upstairs to bed. Jack was an undersized, somewhat skinny Collie, who was typically mischievous and acted like a shark, lurking around for anything to chomp down on, edible or not. He was intelligent in his own ways, but not always terribly smart. At last count, Jack had "eaten" or severely crunched four remote controls for the television and video players. Just two days before leaving on vacation to Tennessee he ate one very nice digital camera.

For all his quirks and idiosyncrasies, Jack was still very much a Collie at heart and he certainly embodied all of the distinguishing characteristics of the breed. Jack exemplified the spirit of a Collie, and this spirit filled the Barnes home and the lives of the members of the Barnes family. While Keith and Linda had started out seeking the perfect pet for their family, they quickly realized that making the decision to spare his life and treat his less than perfect hip was a considerable financial sacrifice that did not exactly occur at the best time, but it did occur at the right time. This canine Christmas present had his share of flaws, as do we all, and that is what made him the perfect gift.

Lana, Will, Sami, Alex, Kevin and Captain Jack!

Kevin L. Brett

Jack In Pictures

Captain Jack
That look spells trouble!
December 2006

Samantha and Jack trying a little soccer.
December 2006

Alexandra wanted to make sure Jack didn't get too cold.
December 2006

Food, water, sleep. What else is there?
December 2006

That infamous first bath! Cleanliness is so overrated!
December 2006

Jack's first winter!
January 2007

0 to 60 in ten leaps!
January 2007

Wow Dad! Is this what it's like in Scotland!
February 2007

All legs and tail!
March 2007

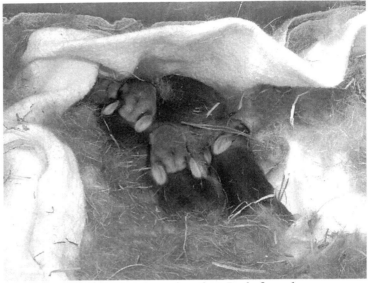

The spring bunnies that Jack found.
April 2007

Jack's entire hip area was shaved and the scar from
the surgery was about seven inches long.
November 2007

One part of the recovery process that Jack didn't mind!
January 2008

Time to maul the girls again! Actually, he's going for her hat.
Jack loves to steal hats.
January 2009

Kevin L. Brett

Piney Branch Lindsay Lad
1979

304

About the Author

Kevin Brett has owned and loved Collies all his life. As a young child, he owned a humongous mahogany Collie named Macintosh. Later, in his teen years, his family had a sable and white Collie, named Piney Branch Lindsay Lad. His current Collie is a tri-color, named Captain Jack.

Kevin is the President and CEO of Kevin Brett Studios, Incorporated of Stafford, Virginia – a media and entertainment company focused on family-oriented books, and videos.

He is a certified martial arts instructor with twenty years of martial arts training and teaching experience. Kevin is also an experienced outdoorsman and survival practitioner and seasoned enterprise architect.

He and his wife Lana Kaye Brett were two of the five co-founders of the United Karate Institute of Self-Defense, Incorporated in Alexandria, Virginia. He has taught martial arts and self-defense combat classes to local law enforcement, military and federal agents, focusing on realistic and practical application of martial arts techniques.

He lives in Stafford, VA with his wife, three children and their mischievous Collie, Captain Jack!

Please send me an email. I'd love to know what you thought of this book, or post a review of it on Amazon.com
Kevin@KevinBrettStudios.com

Kevin L. Brett

For more information and to see other books and videos from Kevin Brett Studios, Incorporated visit us on the web:

Education | Entertainment | Family

www.KevinBrettStudios.com

10204152R0

Made in the USA
Lexington, KY
03 July 2011